"You're not g̶o̶ ̶ ̶ ̶ ̶ ̶ere until you tell me what has you so spooked. Who you're running from."

"It's none of your business," Lindsay began.

Jack moved his face close to hers, his dark eyes shooting enough sparks to singe her with his fury. "It *is* my business. We're connected, you and me, no matter how much you want to deny it."

Lindsay desperately wanted to. But the denial, when it came to her lips, refused to be uttered. She could only stare at him, a wistful sadness twisting inside her. It had been a long time since she'd wanted to be tied to any man. And despite her better judgment, Jack Langley had called to long-dormant feelings in her from the first.

His expression softened marginally. "You're in trouble. Think I can't see that? But you have to trust someone, sometime. I think that someone should be me." He reached up to cup her face in his palm. "Now."

Dear Reader,

One of the riskiest roles on a SWAT incident unit is that of the tactical entry team. If negotiations fail, these personnel are the ones who stage the assault when an armed subject is endangering himself or others. After devising plans for every possible scenario, they must be ready to switch tactics at a moment's notice. Covert entry is the goal. However, if they are discovered in the act of initiating entry, the radio code "Compromise! Compromise! Compromise!" will be sounded. And the risk for injury increases dramatically.

While researching this book, I wondered what sort of character would put himself or herself in that sort of situation on a regular basis. One, I believed, with a strong sense of duty. Someone with a streak of daring, a hint of wildness and an unerring sense of right and wrong. From those musings the hero of this story, Jack Langley, was born.

Like all the characters of the ALPHA SQUAD series, Jack's courage in the face of danger is unflinching. But falling in love brings risk of a far different sort. And when it comes to keeping his woman safe, keeping heart and mind separate on the job becomes increasingly difficult!

I hope you enjoy their story as much as I enjoyed writing it!

All the best,

Kylie Brant

KYLIE BRANT

Terms of Engagement

Silhouette®

Romantic

SUSPENSE

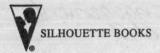

SILHOUETTE BOOKS

Recycling programs
for this product may
not exist in your area.

ISBN-13: 978-0-373-27615-8
ISBN-10:   0-373-27615-X

TERMS OF ENGAGEMENT

Copyright © 2009 by Kimberly Bahnsen

Visit Silhouette Books at www.eHarlequin.com

Printed in U.S.A.

Books by Kylie Brant

Silhouette Romantic Suspense

KYLIE BRANT

is an award-winning author of twenty-two novels. When she's not dreaming up stories of romance and suspense, she works as an elementary teacher for learning disabled students. Kylie has dealt with her newly empty nest by filling the house with even more books, and won't be satisfied until those five vacant bedrooms are full of them!

Kylie invites readers to check out her Web site at www.kyliebrant.com. You can contact her by writing to P.O. Box 231, Charles City, IA 50616 or e-mailing her at kyliebrant@hotmail.com.

In loving memory of my cousin Cheryl, who touched my life and will always live on in my heart.

Acknowledgments:

A special thanks to the amazing Kyle Hiller, Captain, Special Response Team, for taking the time to share your knowledge through your invaluable responses. Your generosity is so greatly appreciated.

Chapter 1

She wasn't a stickler for holiday traditions, but this was just wrong.

Lindsay Bradford pushed aside the sagging string of plastic mistletoe that hung just inside the Blue Lagoon's doorway, only to see a half-naked, drunken Santa seated next to the jukebox. She gave serious consideration to heading back to her apartment. The bar was packed. No one had noticed her yet. If she ducked out now, Dace and Jolie would just give her a hard time tomorrow and that would be the end of it. There was nothing worse than being the last to arrive at a Christmas party, anyway.

Especially a party comprised mostly of *cops*.

Not for the first time, she questioned the wisdom of coming here tonight. Just the thought of being surrounded by a bunch of off-duty policemen had her palms dampening. The fact that the only two friends she'd made in Metro

City had turned out to be detectives was the height of irony. But there was a limit to her appreciation for the ironic.

Some fool saw fit to provide drunk Santa with a mike. If that wasn't a sign, nothing was. She backed slowly toward the door.

"All you lovely ladies out there," he boomed in a surprisingly sexy baritone, "c'mon up here and see me. Don't be shy. If you've been nice girls all year, I've got something for you. And if you're on my naughty list…" He gave an exaggerated wink, eliciting hoots from the audience. "C'mon up here and sit on Santa's lap."

Lindsay rolled her eyes at the feminine squeals of laughter. Several women obviously lacking in discrimination and good taste accepted the invitation and made their way to the dance floor. She took this as her cue to leave.

She wasn't feeling particularly festive, anyway. The palm trees wrapped in rope lighting that lined the California streets didn't evoke the same holiday sentiment as did a decorated, freshly cut pine.

And how incongruous that her longing for home was never so strong as during the holidays. The same time of year she'd chosen to leave Wisconsin and her family behind.

Turning, she headed for the door. But her exit didn't go unnoticed.

"Lindsay! Hey, Lindsay!"

Uh-oh. Busted.

"Lindsay! Over here!"

As she recognized the voice, her stomach dropped. Pasting a plastic smile on her face, she turned to see a disjointed arm waving from a corner booth nearby. It was attached to Mitch Engels, a coworker from the restaurant.

Great. She could do drunk *or* she could do crazy. She wasn't sure she was up to dealing with both.

Resigned, she walked over to his booth, where, unsurprisingly, he was sitting alone.

"So d'ya hear what happened?" He slurred the words as he attempted to smooth his thinning brown hair. "Can't believe it. Neldstrom's such a bastard. Hate that bastard so much."

"Haven't heard anything," she answered truthfully. She'd worked her shift and headed home for a quick shower and change to avoid arriving here awash in eau de fry grease. But she wasn't especially eager to get deluged with the latest in the ongoing battle between Mitch and the restaurant owner.

"He fired me! Said I'd missed too many shifts." Mitch hiccuped wetly. "Didn't even care I'd been sick. That I need the job. He just took me off the schedule and said I was done. At the holidays, too. The bastard."

Drunken Santa began an off-tune rendition of "Blue Christmas." And Lindsay was definitely feeling bluer than she had when she arrived.

"I'm sorry about that, Mitch. Really." If anyone epitomized *victim*, it was Mitch Engels. He was short, plump and prematurely balding, with pale blue eyes magnified by thick, horn-rimmed glasses. He was a nice enough guy, if something of an odd duck. Many at work gave him a wide berth, but Lindsay had always felt sorry for him. She was intimately aware of how it felt to not fit in. "If you need help looking for another job..."

Mitch flung out one hand, knocking his bottle off balance. Only quick reflexes saved Lindsay from a beer bath. "Don't want another job! Want *my* job. You're just like the others at Piper's. You just want me gone."

Lindsay gave a sigh and sat down across from the man,

who looked like he was working himself up to full hissy-fit status. "Mitch." She took his hand in hers, squeezing hard enough to get his attention. "You know that's not true. I want to help you. Why don't you go home and go to bed. You can call me tomorrow and we'll talk about your options, okay?"

He looked pathetically hopeful. "I can call you?"

She wondered if he'd ever heard a female issue that invitation before. Judging from his reaction, probably not. "We'll talk about the job," she emphasized. The last thing she wanted was to shift his bubbling emotions from his unemployment woes to her. "Here's my number." She found a pen and scrap of paper in her purse, and scribbled the cell number she'd given out to few others.

She pushed it across the table toward him. "But you really need to go home now and sleep it off. This place is full of policemen." She doubted that could make him as nervous as it did her. The Blue Lagoon was primarily a cop bar, although its location near Piper's meant some of the restaurant workers were regulars, as well. "You don't need any trouble."

Given the fact that most of the occupants in the bar were probably as loaded as Mitch, she might be overplaying that card, but he accepted the number and her words with alacrity.

"You're right. I'll go." He lurched upward before he'd slid to the end of the booth and nearly toppled face-first onto the tabletop. Lindsay got out and helped him to his feet, gently guiding him toward the door.

"You comin', too?" He swayed, nearly knocking both of them into a harried-looking waitress.

"No, we'll talk tomorrow, remember?" She opened the door for him, ushered him through it. "I'm supposed to be meeting friends here." On the spot she made a commitment to stay; it was better than the alternative. "Grab a cab and get home safely. Talk to you soon."

Before he could muster an answer she withdrew into the noisy bar and shut the door after her. The string of mistletoe hung limply above her, a possible omen of her evening ahead. Certainly it hadn't begun too auspiciously.

Lindsay began to thread her way between tables, looking for Jolie and Dace. The shock of having a pair of cops as friends was secondary to having made friends in Metro City at all. She was usually careful to avoid relationships. It was easier to move on when she wasn't leaving behind anyone she cared about.

And she'd been getting that itchy feeling lately. The one that told her it would soon be time to choose another city. Another job. Another life.

Jolie caught sight of her first and stood, waving her over to a table near the back of the bar. Lindsay felt something inside her lighten. Maybe for tonight she would forget that itchy feeling, and the reason for it. Forget her nonexistent love life, violent past and hopeless future. Spending time with her two favorite people would be the high point of her week.

But when she drew closer to the table and saw a third person seated there, she mentally readjusted her expectations downward. What was drunk Santa doing at their table, and how long before they could get rid of him?

"About time you got here," Jolie scolded cheerfully. "I was about to send Dace to your place to get you."

"I got hung up at work." She exchanged hugs with her two friends.

Dace gave her a quick once-over and grinned as he reseated himself. "You clean up good. Not that the filthy apron and Piper's chef's hat aren't attractive."

Jolie gave him a quick elbow jab. "You look great."

What she looked like in the buttoned-up white shirt and black gauchos, Lindsay knew, was a constipated librarian. She didn't care. Her thrill-seeking days were behind her. And she realized the importance of dressing the part of whatever identity she'd donned for the moment.

With an innocent expression that Lindsay immediately distrusted, Jolie gestured to the stranger and said, "And this shirtless wretch is Jack Langley. I've mentioned him to you, remember?"

Lindsay narrowed a look at her friend. Make that *ex-friend*. This was Jack Langley? The buddy of Dace's that Jolie had mentioned several times wanting her to meet?

Drunk Santa—*Jack*—picked up her hand and sent a caressing thumb skating across her knuckles. A lock of his black hair had escaped from beneath the fur-trimmed Santa hat and fallen rakishly over his forehead. His devil-dark eyes and lopsided grin were guaranteed to melt the coldest of female hearts. Lindsay's remained steely.

Jolie continued, "And this is Lindsay Bradford. Jack, behave. I'm going to get Lindsay a drink. C'mon, Dace."

Dace looked confused. "Why do I have to come?" Jolie grabbed his arm and he stood, long-sufferingly, to trail behind his fiancée.

"I'll bet you're a good girl, Lindsay." Jake raked her with his liquid-coal gaze and a corner of his mouth kicked up. His smile deepened the dimple in his chin. "You look like one. Luckily for you, I still have something in my package for good little girls."

Her brows rose at the transparent euphemism. But then he reached into a paper bag on the table and withdrew a handful of "gifts," setting his offerings in front of her.

She surveyed the slightly wilted fruit slices and paper

umbrellas with a jaundiced look before transferring her attention back to him. "This reminds me. I have a few Christmas disappointments I want to discuss with you. Let's start with that lame Barbie you brought me when I'd specifically asked for a G.I. Joe."

He slapped a hand to his chest, feigning shock. "Those damn elves. They must have mislabeled the package. That's it. Danny the dyslexic elf is getting the ax."

She didn't smile, because it would only encourage him. "Your elves told me working for you is a lot like working in an office. They do all the work and the fat guy in the suit gets all the credit."

He looked amused. And he still hadn't relinquished her hand, despite her discreet tugs. "Half a suit. Half the credit. And they're just smearing my name because they want to unionize." He lowered his voice, and the sexy timbre sent a quick shiver over her nerve endings. "So how about we compare notes before Dace and Jolie get back? I'll tell you what they told me about you if you do the same."

That stopped her short. "They've talked about me to you?" She wasn't sure she liked the sound of that.

"Attractive, even though she plays it down, straitlaced, needs to loosen up a little, good sense of humor, mean at cards," he recited rapidly. "Your turn."

"I'm not sure I remember them mentioning you," she lied. "Are you the one who spent time in prison?"

He gave a loud bark of laughter as Dace and Jolie approached the table again. "Mean, and not only at cards. I like that."

She finally succeeded in wresting her hand free. And found herself curling her fingers into her palm, trapping the heat that lingered. "I have a feeling, Langley, that your 'likes' would fill several dozen little black books."

Jolie set a bottle of Corona in front of Lindsay and sat down again next to Dace. Jack shot the other man a look. "Don't know what you told her about me, but she's got the totally wrong impression."

Dace tipped his bottle to his lips. "She must have. She hasn't run out of here screaming yet."

"Perhaps her impression has something to do with your wardrobe," Jolie put in dryly. "Not everyone finds half-dressed Santas appealing. Go figure."

Jack leaned toward Lindsay, his look of contrition as insincere as that of a ten-year-old altar boy caught sampling the sacramental wine. "The stuffing and the beard were hot. I normally wear shirts. Almost always." He paused, as if to reconsider, then corrected, "At least a lot of the time."

Because she was feeling a little warm herself, Lindsay picked up her beer and drank. And took the time to remind herself of all the reasons she'd sworn off men just like Jack Langley.

He fairly sizzled sex appeal. Anyone with a pair of X chromosomes was bound to respond to it. And it didn't hurt that she had an up close and personal view of his rock-solid build, which had no resemblance to the real Santa's. She'd never given it much thought, but she doubted Jolly Old St. Nick had ever had such broad shoulders, muscled arms, or that washboard belly. Which was a real pity for Mrs. Claus.

But...Lindsay was through looking for thrills. In life, and in men. Safe, solid and secure were the new parameters of her life. And if that equated with dull and dreary...well, at least it kept her alive.

There was nothing remotely safe about Jack Langley.

She set her bottle down and listened politely as the other three talked shop. Despite what she'd said earlier, she remembered everything Jolie and Dace had ever said about the half-naked man sitting next to her. Specifically that he and Dace went way back. That he was a detective like her two friends, assigned to the same SWAT squad. He wasn't a negotiator like Dace and Jolie but was one of the guys who entered the building when an assault became necessary. An adrenaline junkie, she figured, watching him as he conversed. The kind who thrived on danger and risk. The kind who hadn't yet found out that excitement carried its own risk and all too easily could turn deadly.

"Doesn't matter." Jack lifted a shoulder and reached for his beer. And it was annoying to find herself more focused on that expanse of bare skin than on his words. "I'm cleared for duty, and our squad's in line for the next incident. Don't worry about me, I'm ready."

"What happened?" The words were out of Lindsay's mouth before she could stop them.

"He was injured in that explosion at the Metrodome a few months ago," Jolie informed her, her gaze still on Jack. There was a slight furrow between her eyes that indicated Jack hadn't completely alleviated her concern.

"Hurt my leg, but it's healed." Jack picked up one of the sadly wrinkled drink umbrellas from the table in front of him and reached over to tuck it in Lindsay's hair. "Nothing to worry about. But if you'd like to kiss it better, I could be persuaded to drop my Santa britches and show you the wound on my thigh."

The dare in his words was reflected by that wicked glint in his eye. The invitation should have sounded sleazy. But somewhere along the line, probably by grade school, he'd mastered the art of delivering a line with enough humor to engage rather than repel.

Lindsay definitely did not want to find him engaging.

"I'm going to say thanks…but no," she drawled, eliciting laughter from Dace and Jolie. She couldn't prevent a smile at the crestfallen expression Jack affected. He might be—how had Jolie described him?—something of a player, but at least he didn't seem to take himself too seriously. Relaxing a bit, she took another sip of beer. There were worse ways to spend an evening than chatting with friends with a half-naked hunk by her side.

Since looking was about all the action she allowed herself these days, what was the harm in treating herself to a little eye candy for the next couple hours?

Two hours and two beers later, Lindsay had the belated answer to that question.

Harm was an abstract concept.

The time spent in his company had only fanned her slumbering hormones to an unwelcome simmer, which was definitely a waste, because there was no way she was going to indulge them. It would have been simpler if she could dismiss Jack as just another good-looking guy with a smooth line and easy banter. But the affection Jolie and Dace had for him was evident. And he was amusing, whether trading good-natured barbs with Dace or directing humorous asides to her.

It was almost enough to lull her well-honed instincts into believing Jack Langley was harmless, and that would have been a mistake. Lindsay was perceptive enough to see the toughness beneath the charm and smart enough to steer clear of both.

To distract herself from the stab of regret that thought brought, she focused on her friends across the table. Jolie was as guarded as Lindsay was herself, which was why it had taken weeks after their initial meeting outside the restaurant for Lindsay to learn the woman's occupation. By then it had been too late for that inner shrill of alarm. They'd been solidly on the way to becoming friends. Jolie had told Lindsay enough about her and Dace's past to make Lindsay doubly happy for the plans they were making for their future. The thought of not being around for their wedding this spring brought a pang, but there was always the possibility that she could come back for it.

Panic stabbed through her at the errant thought. Once she moved on, she never went back. Not ever. She didn't use the same identity twice or even stay in the same state. Doing the unexpected had kept her alive this long. She couldn't alter her strategy now.

Troubled, she rubbed at the condensation on the bottle with her thumb. This was why it was best to have no lasting relationships. Ties elicited emotion. Emotion fogged logic. Made it difficult to leave and start over.

But starting over had long since lost the appeal it had once held.

"Jolie says you're a cook at Piper's." Jack's husky baritone sounded in her ear. "Maybe you'd like to go out somewhere you can order a meal you don't have to prepare." At her silence, he lifted a lazy black brow. "I'll wear a shirt, I promise. And I do have clothes that aren't red and trimmed with fur."

"For the department's sake, that's good to know." She met his gaze, far more tempted than she should have been. "But I don't think so."

He studied her. "Still holding that Barbie–G.I. Joe screwup against me? I can make that up to you this Christmas. I won't let the elves near the package this time. Promise."

Her lips curved. He was far too likable for his own good. "I'm not going to sleep with you." Her hormones sent up a disappointed chorus. But she didn't make decisions based on her hormones these days, so they were easily ignored. Mostly. "And I'm not your type, anyway."

"What type do you think that is?"

"The type that will sleep with you."

He grinned, a quick flash of white teeth. "And if I reserve the right to try and change your mind about that?"

"Then you'll be wasting both our time." With more regret than she cared to show, she stood. "Will you excuse me for a few minutes?" Without waiting for a response, she picked up her purse and wound her way through the full tables to the restroom at the back of the bar. She fully expected Jack to be gone when she returned to the table. He didn't strike her as the type of guy to hang around after a rejection.

And she'd been issuing rejections for far too long for this one to be causing her so much regret.

But even though she lingered in the restroom far longer than necessary, Jack was still seated at their table when Lindsay came out. Seeing him, she stopped, indecisive. Maybe he needed a little more time to grow bored and move on. As if in response to her thoughts, a woman wearing what looked to be the top of Jack's Santa outfit sauntered over to him and draped an arm around his neck, planting an enthusiastic kiss on his mouth.

Saved by the Santa slut. Turning, she made her way for the back door, intent on delaying her return to the table a bit longer. Give him the amount of time it took to get a breath of fresh air, and he'd be gone. She'd lay odds on it.

And she was suddenly desperately in need of fresh air.

Moments later she was standing outside in the shadows. After the press of bodies in the bar the solitude was a welcome reprieve.

Resting her shoulders against the back of the building,

she tipped her head back and studied the star-studded sky. She'd always liked looking at the stars. Maybe when she left she'd head to Wyoming. With the wide-open spaces there, the expanse of sky would be magnificent.

But wait. Wyoming didn't have many big cities. She always felt safer in cities. More anonymous. It was easier to blend in and escape notice.

It was imperative that Lindsay escape notice.

The door swung open and she turned her head, instantly wary. A couple stumbled out the door, laughing breathlessly. She opened her mouth to alert them to her presence, but at that moment the man pulled the woman into his arms and they exchanged a long, heated kiss.

Great. She jerked her gaze away. Playing voyeur to an alcohol-fueled couple with loosened inhibitions was definitely not what she'd had in mind when she'd slipped outside. She began to inch away, intent on returning to the bar.

"No." The woman's voice was still laughing. Lindsay moved a little faster, still hoping to escape detection. Then a moment later, "No, Rick. Stop it. I said—"

There was the unmistakable sound of a slap and a cry of pain. Lindsay jerked around to peer through the darkness.

"Bitch." The two were scuffling now, the woman struggling to get away. "Think you can tease me all night and not come through when we're alone?"

"I wasn't teasing—"

"Well you aren't now, because you're going to…"

"Let her go." Fury snapped through Lindsay's veins, fogging good sense. She strode toward the couple, grabbed the man's shoulder. "She said no."

With a suddenness that took her off guard, he turned around and gave her a shove that sent her sprawling. "Get lost, bitch. Unless you want to be next. Believe me, I got plenty here to satisfy both of you."

The other woman screamed as the man hauled her against him, moving her deeper into the shadows. His mouth ground over hers, halting her protests.

Lindsay picked herself up and stumbled to the back door again, intent on getting help. If she didn't hurry, the couple could be gone by the time she got back. If he had a car or a place nearby, no one would catch him in time.

She rushed inside, the barrage of sound from the bar blasting her anew. The crowd seemed to have gotten thicker. She tried to squeeze through, her actions frantic, but made little headway.

An idea occurred and she pulled out her cell phone. She could call Jolie even faster and alert her to bring help, while she went out again and—

A hand touched her shoulder and she nearly jumped out of her skin. Jack stood next to her, his figure solid and re-assuring. He bent his head, pitching his voice loud enough to be heard over the din. "Where have you been? Jolie was getting worried."

"A woman needs help outside."

He shook his head, an expression of puzzlement on his face. The jukebox was blaring out the latest Dixie Chicks tune at ear-deafening levels. "What?"

"Come with me!" He may not have understood her words, but he couldn't misunderstand her hand on his arm, tugging him in her wake.

Bursting outside again, she halted, scanning the area. Her stomach plummeted when she didn't see anyone in the vicinity. "I don't see them."

"What, my reindeer? I have them parked out front."

Lindsay headed deeper into the alley, calling over her

shoulder, "There was a man out here trying to force himself on a woman. When I tried to stop him he shoved me down. I'm afraid he might have taken her somewhere no one will find them."

"He touched you?" Jack's tone changed from affable to threatening with a swiftness that might have alarmed her if she weren't already so distracted. "What'd he look like?"

But Lindsay was running ahead, the pain in her knees from the scrapes she'd gotten barely registering. The alley ended in a T. She rounded the corner to her right. If it hadn't been for the sound of the woman's muffled sobs, she would have missed the couple hidden in a doorway.

She hefted her purse as she ran toward them. The two rolls of quarters she always carried in it seemed woefully inadequate. But they were all she had since she'd left her gun back at the apartment.

"You like games, Sheila?" She could barely make out the man's panted words. He had a forearm across the woman's throat, his free hand pulling up her skirt. "Let's play some games."

His choice of words arrowed deep into her subconscious. Summoned an echo of a voice she'd thought buried for good. *You think this is a game? Well, maybe it is. But it isn't one you're going to win.*

A quick shudder snaked down Lindsay's spine as she shook off the memory. She closed the distance between them at a run. The man looked over his shoulder, a snarl on his lips when he saw Lindsay. She swung her purse with all her might and nailed him squarely in the face.

There was a sickening crack. He howled, cursing, turning around to make a grab for her. She felt her shirt rip and struggled wildly to free herself, but he maintained his grasp. When he hit the ground, so did she.

He was on her in an instant, flipping her over and rolling atop her. She raised her knee up sharply into his crotch, her fingernails going for his face, heard him yelp.

"Goddammit!" He reared an arm back and struck her across the cheek with enough force to send lights wheeling beneath her eyelids. A moment later, he was gone.

Dazed, she tried to sit, the movement making her nauseous. She became dimly aware of the sounds around her. Grunts and curses. A soft sobbing. The instantly recognizable sound of flesh hitting flesh.

Without grace she stood up, swaying. It was a moment before she could stagger over to the woman—Sheila—who was huddled in the doorway. Lindsay went on her knees next to her, slipping an arm around her shoulder. "It's all right. It's over."

She craned her neck to see what was happening several yards away. Jack had the man against the wall and was hammering him with methodical punishing blows.

A moment later she realized the stranger's struggles had grown feeble, and she left the woman's side to lurch across the distance and grab Jack's arm. "Stop."

She could feel the ice-cold fury emanating from him. The iron muscles in his arm quivered like a racehorse at the starting gate. "Jack," she said softly. Something in her voice must have reached him and he looked at her. She watched the sheen of rage slowly dissipate from his eyes, and then he released the man, who crumpled in a heap.

"You're bleeding," he observed tersely, his gaze raking her form.

Surprised, she looked down. Her shirt was in tatters, and there was blood soaking it. She gathered the remnants of the garment around her. "It's not mine."

He reached out a finger and tipped her chin up so he

could study her. Whatever he saw in her face must have reassured him, because something in his expression eased. He looked past her then. "Give Jolie or Dace a call. Get them out here." He walked by her to go to the aid of the woman who was even now struggling to her feet. "And if that scumbag back there so much as moves, let me know."

With shaking fingers, Lindsay punched in Jolie's number, relayed Jack's message and interrupted her friend's questions with a terse, "Just get out here. Bring Dace."

When she glanced his way, Jack looked like he had things under control with Sheila, so Lindsay edged nearer the man, who had risen to a sitting position, both hands clapped over his face.

"You broke my damn nose, you freaking whore." His voice was muffled. "My lawyer will sue your ass. You'll pay for butting into something that's none of your business. Langley, too."

"You got off easy," she responded bluntly. "And your lawyer is going to be too busy defending you from attempted rape and assault charges to worry about me." Hearing the sounds of footsteps running toward them, she turned to see Dace turn the corner into the alley, Jolie and a woman she didn't recognize on his heels.

Relief coursed through her. "Look, it's the cavalry."

Dace stopped at her side while the two women continued down the alley to help Jack with the injured woman. Hauling the man up by one arm, Dace growled, "What the hell have you been up to now, Fallon?"

"Me?" Fallon's voice would have sounded indignant if he weren't speaking through a broken nose. "Sheila and I came out for a few minutes of privacy and the next thing I know that bitch over there is jumping me. And then Langley gets into the act. You tell him I'm pressing assault charges."

"Tell him yourself." Dace gave him a little push. "I'm parked in front. Let's go downtown."

"I need a doctor!" Fallon protested.

"Ava and I will take Sheila to the hospital." Jolie strode up, eyes hard. "I'll get her statement there, then meet you at the precinct."

Dace nodded then led the man away. Jolie and Lindsay returned to where Jack was waiting with Sheila and Ava. Quickly Jolie introduced Lindsay to Ava, who was another member of their SWAT squad.

"I can't thank you enough," Sheila said shakily to Lindsay when the introductions were over. "If you hadn't been there he would have raped me. I never wanted... I told him no...."

"And I heard you. This isn't your fault."

"Jack, see Lindsay home, will you?" Jolie's next words halted both their protests. "Sheila will be more comfortable with Ava and me right now than you. And I don't want Lindsay to be alone."

Sliding a glance to Lindsay, Jack nodded. "All right. We'll be downtown as soon as she gets changed."

The adrenaline had faded, leaving Lindsay feeling sapped and spent. She hugged her arms tight around her body and willed her knees to remain locked to support her increasingly wobbly legs. She was only half-aware that Jolie, Ava and Sheila had gone when Jack approached her again.

She strove to straighten when he surveyed her critically.

"You must have gotten a few good swings in."

Her entire body began shaking. "I can't take credit for that. You're the one who stopped him."

"You're in shock." He hauled her to his chest and wrapped his arms around her.

"I'm not." She wasn't weak. She despised weakness. But she couldn't will away the shudders racing up and down her body.

"Okay, maybe you're cold." Knowing that he was merely humoring her didn't make her feel any better. "And me without a shirt to offer you."

For a moment, just a moment, Lindsay allowed herself to lean against him. His skin was hot despite the chilly air. She could feel his heart thudding beneath her ear, the steady sound comforting. For the briefest of moments, she felt completely, totally safe.

The sensation was foreign enough to have her stepping out of his arms. If she'd learned anything in the last three years, it was that she couldn't depend on anyone else to protect her.

She liked her chances better on her own.

Avoiding his gaze, she folded the remains of her shirt around herself and held it in place by crossing her arms over her chest. "Since I'm not feeling particularly festive anymore, I'll think I'll head home."

"Good idea. I know that lowlife's name. Rick Fallon. He's a dispatcher from the Eighth Precinct, I think. We'll get you cleaned up, then we'll join Dace downtown. Your statement will help support Sheila's. Fallon will try to claim that what was going on out here was consensual."

"No!" The strength of her protest surprised them both. Working to keep the panic from her voice, she forced an even tone. "I wouldn't be much help. I didn't see a lot." Making statements would require ID, wouldn't it? ID that couldn't stand up to close scrutiny.

He frowned, studying her carefully. But rather than pushing harder, he just said mildly, "Let's just worry about you right now. Maybe we should have a doctor check you out."

"I just need to go home." Bending down, she tried to pick up the contents of her purse, which had spilled out sometime during the altercation. It was slow going, since she couldn't let go of her shirt.

Jack crouched down and scooped everything up and returned it to her purse, holding up the rolls of quarters with a cocked brow. "Hope you nailed him with these."

"I did." Not, she recalled, that it had slowed him down much. When he handed her back her purse, she pulled out her cell phone. "I'm going to call a taxi. Thanks for riding to the rescue."

"Don't bother calling for a cab." He plucked the cell out of her hand, and, placing a palm on the small of her back, guided her down the alley. "You're in luck. Like I said, I've got my sleigh and eight bored reindeer parked right out front."

Chapter 2

Jack Langley was a hard man to say no to. Impossible, actually.

Within moments he had Lindsay herded into the front seat of a sporty, low-slung car and had elicited directions to her place. He'd turned on the heater, but the blast of warm air wasn't having much effect on the shivers still skating over her skin.

Her teeth were chattering. She gripped her arms more tightly across her chest, vaguely disquieted that she had so little control over her body's reaction.

With a clutch in her stomach, she realized her response had less to do with the attack and everything to do with the memory the stranger had unwittingly summoned.

You even think about betraying me and I'll kill you. Are you hearing me?

She slipped farther down in the seat, battling nausea.

Every time she started to believe she'd begun to put the past behind her, something happened to show her just how solid a grip it still wielded. She'd run over two thousand miles but nothing had really changed at all. Lindsay could still hear the menace in Niko Rassi's voice, still feel the grip of his fingers around her neck.

And she still had no doubt it was only a matter of time before he caught up with her. Until she was resting at the bottom of a riverbed, just like her friends.

Her cheek throbbed and she raised a hand to it, wincing when she touched it.

"What's wrong?" Jack's voice was sharp with concern. And his vision must be equally sharp to have seen her expression of pain in the darkened front seat.

"I'm fine. I just need some ice. Guys like him know how to hit a woman just hard enough to avoid serious damage." Niko had mastered the art of the backhanded slap, too. That was only the beginning of the many unpleasant discoveries she'd made about him.

"If you have that much experience with guys who hit women, you're hanging around the wrong kind of men."

"Tell me about it," she muttered. There was something in his voice she couldn't identify, but his words struck a chord. They didn't get any more *wrong* than Niko Rassi. They didn't get any deadlier.

A wave of fatalism swamped her, a sensation she usually fended off during long, sleepless nights spent staring at the ceiling. Niko might not have found her yet, but in a manner of speaking he'd already won. He'd robbed her of any sort of real life. Robbed her of any chance of family. Had her constantly watching over her shoulder. She knew him well enough to realize how much he'd enjoy that.

To distract herself from that line of thought, she asked, "What does Ava do on the squad?"

"She's a marksman. Her nickname's Cold Shot." A tinge of humor entered Jack's voice. "You're only slightly less dangerous than she is. Fallon had a lucky escape."

Moments later Jack slowed the car to a stop. "Looks like a nice house."

"The house *is* nice. I live over the garage." Releasing her seat belt, Lindsay opened the door. "I appreciate the ride—" she began.

But Jack was already out of the car. Slowly, Lindsay rounded the hood, mentally rehearsing a way to get rid of him. All she really wanted right now was a hot bath and a cold pack for her face. Given the contents of her apartment, she'd be making due with a tepid shower in the minuscule stall and a package of frozen peas held to her cheek.

"Like I said, thanks for everything..." Her second attempt was no more successful than the first.

"You're not getting rid of me until I see your injuries in the light and make sure you don't need to go to the ER. So save your breath and get your key out." Open-mouthed, Lindsay could only stare as Jack strode ahead of her to ascend the narrow exterior stairway leading to her apartment.

It wasn't much. Jack threw a quick, all-encompassing look around the small space. The fresh paint on the walls only made the secondhand furniture look rattier. There was a sagging easy chair and a fairly comfortable-looking daybed situated around a small TV in one corner. A midget-size kitchenette was placed opposite, with a small countertop eating area and a couple doors that had to open to closets or a bathroom.

But it wasn't the meagerness of the space that struck him. It was the total absence of any personal items in it.

There were no pictures on the walls or on the tops of the mismatched end tables. There weren't any of the useless things women were forever hanging up or setting around for a clumsy guy to knock into. No magazines. No books. No CDs or, for that matter, anything to play them on.

"How long have you lived here?"

"Six months or so."

So she hadn't just moved in. Wasn't in the middle of unpacking her things. Lindsay Bradford didn't have anything to unpack. His curiosity deepened.

She brushed by him and went to one of the doors and pulled it open. Looking past her, he saw a bathroom barely big enough to turn around in. She stepped inside and swung the door shut behind her. But it didn't latch and swung open again several inches. He was honorable enough to avert his eyes, male enough to resent needing to.

Half a dozen scenarios occurred to him. Was she recently divorced? Jolie and Dace hadn't mentioned an ex, but maybe they didn't know about one. Or maybe she'd just gotten out of a bad relationship. Yeah, that could be it. Maybe he'd been abusive. That would explain the comment she'd made in the car.

He found he didn't much like the idea of someone raising a hand to her. Hell, he'd still be beating on Fallon for doing so if Lindsay hadn't stopped him.

A hard smile crossed his lips when he thought of what the man had in store for him. His bruises were going to be the least of his worries. Jack had heard rumors that the guy had a reputation for roughing up women. There might even be a misdemeanor or two in his past. Once he convinced Lindsay to make a statement backing up the woman's complaint, Fallon's career was in the trash heap. It was about damn time.

Second nature had him crossing to the window in the kitchenette, checking its security. Cool air seeped in at the seam where the sash met the sill. Frowning, he jiggled the window. Despite the lock, it rattled easily. A five-year-old armed with a toy screwdriver could jimmy it open in two minutes flat.

"You need to have the landlord spring for a screen. And a new lock for the window," he called over his shoulder. "Or else I could just…" The words died in his throat.

From this angle, he could see her in profile through the opening of the bathroom door. She'd stripped off the ripped shirt and the wide pants. Once again it occurred to him that Lindsay Bradford was a study of contrasts. She dressed as sedate as a nun, but what nun wore a matching black-and-white-striped bra and panties? What nun had a silver hoop piercing her navel and a tiny tattoo of a butterfly on one smooth shoulder blade?

She turned around to reach for something, saw him watching her and froze. The oxygen abruptly backed up in his lungs.

Because a nun wouldn't look at him with naked desire in her expression, either. Desire that he fully, achingly reciprocated.

The moment spun out. Neither of them moved. Hell, he couldn't move. Couldn't breathe. Could only stare like a lovesick teenager. Want like a sex-starved hermit.

An instant later she stepped closer to the door and closed it firmly.

The pent-up air in his lungs released. He turned back

to the window, shaken. He needed to get out of here. Lindsay had made it pretty damn clear in the bar that she wasn't interested in casual entanglements. And while ordinarily he might test her resolve a bit, he sure as hell wasn't going to do it after what she'd been through tonight.

And if that left his more insistent body parts aching, it was too damn bad.

To distract himself, he crossed to the apartment door, yanked it open and jogged down the steps toward his car. The blast of cool air was welcome against his heated skin. It was time to back the hell up. His response to the woman was all out of whack.

Opening the trunk lid with his remote, he reached in for his toolbox and shut the lid again. He headed back toward the steps to her apartment. Okay. The lady had had a rough night. He'd fix her window, make sure she was steady on her feet and head in to the precinct alone. She could make her statement in the morning. Maybe if it wasn't too late, he'd even head back to the Blue Lagoon. The bar was filled with females who would be far more interested than Lindsay had been earlier.

And sometime between now and then, he'd work on summoning a little interest in them in return. Because he wasn't a man who welcomed complications in his life. And if there was one thing Lindsay Bradford had written all over her, it was *complication,* in big, bold capital letters.

He was hammering the second of two nails into her window sash when he heard her raised voice behind him. "What the heck are you doing?"

Giving the nail a final blow with the hammer, he turned. "Making sure some lowlife doesn't decide to come in your window."

She was swathed in a white zip-up terry-cloth robe that

covered her from throat to feet. There was nothing remotely sexy about the garment. It was recalling what lay beneath it that was giving him a bad moment. Scowling, he passed her to squat before the toolbox, replacing the hammer and locking the lid.

She eyed the window dubiously. "I don't think there's much danger of that. He'd need a pair of stilts at this height."

"Or a ladder. After tonight you shouldn't be surprised at how far stupidity and hormones take some guys." She paled, and he mentally kicked himself. Like she needed a reminder of the altercation earlier.

Deliberately lightening the mood, he added, "Although once bad guys get a look at what you did to Fallon, I'd imagine they'd be steering clear of you." The small smile those words elicited had heat coiling low in his belly.

"I think you inflicted the worst damage there."

He surveyed her without trying to be obvious about it. She'd showered, and her dark, wet hair was combed straight back off her face to fall below her shoulders. There was already a mark blooming on one chiseled cheekbone. But her eyes were clear, unclouded by the shadows he'd seen there in the car. They were cat-green, unusual for her coloring.

And he was losing it completely if he was standing here mooning over the color of a woman's eyes.

"You should get something on your face." He went to the doll-size refrigerator and opened the freezer. The only ice was in trays, so he grabbed the bag of frozen peas and wrapped it in the kitchen towel that had been draped neatly over the faucet. He walked back and handed it to her. "I'm sure Jolie will come if you need someone to stay with you tonight."

She was already shaking her head. "I'm fine. She's got enough to deal with tonight. I'll talk to her tomorrow."

Since she seemed steady enough now, he figured it was as good a time as any to broach the subject of her statement. He backed up, propping a hip against the kitchen counter and folding his arms. "Making a statement isn't difficult. I can walk you through the process if you—"

"I already told you, I'm not interested."

Lindsay saw Jack's gaze narrow and knew she was going to get an argument. She'd already learned that he didn't take no for an answer.

But this time he'd have to. If there was one thing she'd learned, it was that cops required ID for *everything*. And while hers *might* get only cursory examination, she couldn't afford to take that chance. She'd made sure no trace of her name showed up on any public record for the last three years. Her caution had kept her alive. She wasn't about to start making mistakes now.

Jack crossed one foot in front of the other, and for a moment she found herself distracted by the action. He'd strayed from the Santa uniform with the boots. They were a deep brown rather than black, with richly tooled leather that screamed *designer*. They probably cost what she paid in six months' rent.

"I know the guy. He's got a reputation with women, but so far no one has taken the step to make him pay for his actions. If Sheila Jennings presses charges—and it sure sounded like she planned to—she's going to need your statement to back hers up. Otherwise he'll spin it that she was willing, and he'll walk again. And then he'll do the same thing to some other woman."

His words had her nerves congealing in a greasy tangle in her stomach. If Jack hadn't come outside with her, the outcome of the evening would have been far different. She would have suffered far worse injuries than a bruised cheek, and Sheila... She swallowed hard, thinking what might have happened to the woman. But she couldn't focus on that now. And she couldn't allow herself to be manipulated into feeling guilty about a woman she didn't know and possible future victims.

She was already carrying all the guilt she could live with.

"Save your breath. I've made up my mind and you're not going to change it."

The frustration on his face was easy to read. "Dammit, Lindsay..."

"Dammit, Jack..." She crossed her arms to mimic his stance. Well, not exactly, since her chest wasn't bare. And her arms weren't bulging with all sorts of interesting muscles. But he wasn't going to intimidate her, regardless.

He gave a curt nod. "I'll let you sleep on it. Maybe when Jolie talks to you tomorrow you'll change your mind."

Although she didn't relish the upcoming conversation, she shook her head. "I won't."

His jaw tightened, and the toughness she'd noted earlier was not so hidden now. "I don't think I've ever met anyone as stubborn as you."

"Then you haven't looked in the mirror lately."

For a moment she thought her reckless tongue had gotten her in trouble again. His face darkened and he looked like a man struggling to leash his temper. Then he pushed away from the counter and grabbed her purse, digging inside it to take out her cell phone.

Her brows rose, but she wisely chose to keep her objections to herself. He took his out, too, and pressed keys in rapid succession on both. Then he flipped them shut and dropped hers back into her purse. "I added my number in case you come to your senses before tomorrow night."

His number? The thought suffused her with heat. And

far more temptation than she was up to battling right now. No doubt he'd coded her number into his directory, as well. "What's tomorrow night?"

"Our dinner date. I'll pick you up at eight."

He bent to pick up his toolbox before heading to the door.

She was speechless for one long moment. And no, that absolutely was *not* interest stirring inside her. "Wait a minute." She followed him to the door. "I'm not having dinner with you. I thought I made that clear earlier at the bar."

He turned to face her. Somewhere he'd lost the Santa hat, which just made that sardonic cock of his brow more noticeable. "You really think you're going to win two arguments with me tonight?"

"One has absolutely nothing to do with the other. And we both know you'd just spend the entire evening trying to convince me to make that statement."

He rested a shoulder against the door. She wondered fleetingly if he ever stood up straight. His pose called attention to his lean hips and narrow waist, though the baggy red pants made it impossible to make out the line of his thigh…. Realizing where her gaze had gone, she jerked it upward and saw a fleeting expression of humor in Jack's eyes.

"That's not true," he said mildly. "Because willing or not, you will be interviewed by an officer about the scene at the Blue Lagoon. I'm going to spend dinner trying to persuade you to sleep with me."

She dropped the makeshift ice pack on the counter and glared at him impotently. "I have no intention of sleeping with you!"

"Then I have my work cut out for me."

Aggravated, she drew a breath. Her emotions felt like they'd been on an out-of-control carousel tonight. But right now they were settled solidly in annoyance. "This is exactly why I don't like cops. They're pushy, and devious and untrustworthy." And some were corrupt, placing their own greed above others' lives.

"We'll discuss your grievances with the department tomorrow night, too."

She angled her chin, belatedly insulted. "What makes you think I'm free tomorrow night?"

"Piper's closes at six, and Jolie and Dace claim you have no social life. So tomorrow night, I'm it."

Jolie and Dace had told him she had no social life? Mortification mingled with irritation. Just because it was true— just because it was her choice—didn't mean it didn't sting.

He cut through her momentary silence by commanding, "Come over here."

Instantly wary, she remained where she was. "Why?"

"So you can lock the door behind me." He jerked his head toward the ice pack she'd left on the counter. "Then for the rest of the night keep ice on that cheek. Twenty minutes on, twenty minutes off. It's going to start hurting once you fall asleep and the numbness wears off. You're going to want to take a pain reliever before you turn in."

In face of the genuine concern in his voice Lindsay felt her ire fade away. And that was perhaps the most lethal part of Langley's attractiveness. It would be easier to ignore his sexual magnetism if he wasn't so darn likable.

She was reminded again of what he'd done for her that night, and she felt something inside her soften further. "I will. Thank you."

He lifted a shoulder. "Hey, it's Fallon who should be thanking me. If I hadn't shown up when I did you probably would have crippled him."

The suggestion was outrageously untrue and guaranteed to make her smile.

He sobered, studying her intently. "I'd feel better if someone stayed with you tonight. Are you sure you don't want to call Jolie?"

"I'm really okay," she assured him. And she was. The events of the night had rattled her, but she'd regained her equilibrium. And there was satisfaction to be had from knowing that for once she hadn't been too late. That she'd helped save a woman from certain trauma.

On impulse, she closed the distance between them, went up on tiptoe and brushed a kiss across his cheek. "But thank you. For everything."

She went to step back. Found it impossible. Jack's hand had slipped behind her nape, his thumb tilting her chin up. There was a hint of a smile in his voice, on his lips, when he said huskily, "You're welcome."

But she detected no amusement when his mouth covered hers. What she tasted was heat. It transferred from his lips to hers and sent corresponding spirals spinning through her veins. He wasn't a man to miss an opportunity, she reminded herself. But she'd invited this one, hadn't she, the moment she gotten this close to him.

Maybe she hadn't changed as much as she'd hoped.

Because responding to his latent sexuality meant she hadn't completely conquered her desire for excitement. Returning the hard pressure of his mouth meant she hadn't outgrown her taste for a little danger.

That should have dismayed her. Terrified her. But those weren't the emotions careening through her system right now. He kissed with the same lazy self-assurance that was so much a part of him. With just a hint of wickedness that invited her to be wicked with him.

And Lindsay was tempted. When his tongue swept inside her mouth, she met it with her own, relishing the dark flavor that traced through her system. Desire rose quickly, whipping her blood to churning white caps.

Emboldened, she leaned into him, taking the kiss deeper as she raised her hands to his chest. Her fingers flexed against the hard muscled planes, a purr of feminine satisfaction in the back of her throat. His chest was just as solid as it looked, with all sorts of intriguing angles and hollows where sinew met bone. She had the overpowering urge to tear her mouth from his and test one hard pec with her teeth.

She didn't recall ever feeling this fever in her blood that stripped away the caution she'd learned to live by. This scorching heat was its own kind of seduction for a woman used to keeping her own wild nature tamed.

Jack Langley made her want to unleash it. And that made him far more dangerous than she had first assumed.

The realization had Lindsay reluctantly tearing her mouth from his, evading his lips when they would have lured her back.

Each of them drew a deep, shuddering breath. If he said anything, did anything, Lindsay couldn't be certain she'd have the strength of will to resist him.

When he spoke, his voice was an octave lower than usual. "Don't forget to lock up after me."

She had to force herself to back up a few steps to allow him space to pull the door open. Clenching her hands at her sides, she managed to let him walk through it without hauling him back inside.

But it was a long moment before she could manage to do as he directed and lock the door behind him.

"You went to see Neldstrom?" Coming fully awake, Lindsay sat up in bed, her cell phone clutched to her ear. "Mitch, I wish you hadn't done that."

Early-morning light slanted through the blinds covering the lone window. She didn't know what time it was when she'd taken Mitch's call. But Piper's opened at 6:00 a.m. Mitch hadn't wasted any time.

"He humiliated me. In front of everyone." There was an unfamiliar note of rage in the man's voice, layered under the mortification. "He looked me right in the eye and dumped the plate of food down my shirt. Poured juice on my head. Said I must be slower than he thought if I didn't get the message."

Lindsay's jaw clenched. The owner of Piper's, Bill Neldstrom, was something of an ass. She'd seem him lose his temper before. The episode with Mitch hadn't been his first. But he paid in cash and didn't require references when hiring. That had made him an attractive employer for Lindsay.

"You didn't deserve that, Mitch. He's a jerk. You'll find a better job. With a nicer boss."

"No one did a thing to stop him. No one said a thing about it." Mitch's voice was tinged with bitterness. "Alex just smirked at me. Like maybe I had it coming."

Bringing a hand up to rub her temple, Lindsay grazed her cheekbone and flinched. "I'm sorry that happened. Bill had no right to treat you that way, and I'll tell him that."

There was a beat of silence. Then, "You don't work today, do you?"

"No." Thank God, she mentally added. Various aches she'd been unaware of last night were making themselves known now, a regular little chorus of pain. "But when I see him tomorrow…"

"Don't worry about it. Bill is going to get his one of these days."

"Guys like him usually do." She hoped her words sounded more certain than she felt. Her experience was quite the opposite. Innocents were destroyed while evil flourished. And waiting for justice could take a lifetime. "But I'm free this afternoon. How about if I buy some newspapers and you and I can go through the want ads? That would show Bill, if you had a new job lined up in just a few days."

"Maybe another time." Mitch sounded preoccupied. "Promise you won't go talk to him today."

Stifling a yawn, Lindsay lowered herself gingerly to a prone position again. That was a promise she'd have no trouble keeping. This would be her first day off all week. "I won't."

"Good. I'll talk to you later."

"All right. And, Mitch? We *will* find you a better job."

Once the call had been disconnected, she checked the time on the phone. Past nine. But she was in no hurry to get up. Jack had been right. Her face had throbbed during the night, making it difficult to fall asleep. She was unwilling to admit that there had been any other cause for her sleeplessness. Unless it had been mortification at the struggle it had taken not to jump the man's bones before he'd walked out the door.

Pulling a pillow over her face, she sought to shut out that particular memory. It was humbling to discover that despite her conviction otherwise, she hadn't changed much at all over the last three years. She could switch her name and her lifestyle, dress in another manner, act different...but she hadn't tamed her nature at all. She'd merely subdued it.

All it had taken was the sex appeal and lethal aura of one man to entice that wildness back to the surface. That meant she still was drawn to excitement. She still found herself tempted by risk.

She *had* to cancel dinner that evening.

She hadn't completely lost her mind, those few minutes in Jack's arms to the contrary. She'd learned caution the hard way. She'd learned to listen to her instincts.

And they warned her not to make a mistake with Jack Langley. If she couldn't trust herself with the man, it made sense to avoid him altogether.

Pushing aside the niggle of disappointment, she reached for her cell, intent on getting it over with. It rang in her palm. Recognizing the number, her stomach plummeted. But she knew better than to not answer it.

"Lindsay, cancel any plans you've made and get down to the restaurant." As usual, Bill Neldstrom didn't give her a chance to speak. "Chang just went home sick, and Sarah's in San Diego for the weekend. I've got my hands full here, and I can't do the cooking and supervise the waitstaff, too."

Everything inside her rebelled. "Bill, I haven't had a day off all week. You promised you wouldn't call me in. Just yesterday, in fact."

"Well, I didn't know that Chang was going to catch a bug, did I?" His tone was testy. "You can have a different day off."

"When?" She wasn't feeling particularly charitable, especially after hearing about his run-in with Mitch. "You've fired the grill cook and Sarah's gone for a week. Tell me when I'm going to get some time off, Bill, especially with Chang out sick."

"You want to be off permanently? I can arrange that pretty damn easily."

The temptation to shove his job down his throat was almost overwhelming. Lindsay sat up in bed, jamming her free hand through her hair. But rent was due next week. And it wouldn't hurt to have a little extra put aside for when she moved on. Telling Neldstrom off would have to wait until then.

"I should at least get overtime for this." But she was already swinging her legs over the side of the daybed.

His laugh sounded genuinely amused. "Sure. You bring in a Social Security number and you can get all those Department of Labor perks. Now move your ass. You'd better be here in thirty minutes."

She took a small measure of satisfaction in disconnecting the call and hurling the phone down on the pillow. Neldstrom was a miserable worm and a poor excuse for a human being. Unfortunately, he had the upper hand and delighted in wielding it. He was one she'd be all too happy to leave behind when she left Metro City.

Striding to her closet, she pulled open the door and grabbed a pair of jeans and a T-shirt. It would take nearly the entire allotted time just to walk to the nearest bus stop and make it down to Piper's.

Dressing quickly, she abruptly remembered she'd been about to call Jack. With a mental shrug, she wiggled into her jeans and fastened them. She could call when she had a free minute at work. It would give her a chance to prepare for the conversation.

She had a feeling she was going to need all her wits about her when she talked to him.

Chapter 3

"Bill talked you into coming in, huh?" Song, a Eurasian woman with the size and build of a twelve-year-old boy, cast a sympathetic if harried glance Lindsay's way as she entered the kitchen.

"Man's got a silver tongue," she acknowledged wryly, stowing her purse beneath one of the stainless-steel counters. She waved hello to Bobby, the teenager manning the dishwashers, and scanned the fluttering tickets in the order window. She gave a mental sigh. Any thoughts of getting out before closing abruptly dissipated.

"Sorry." Song expertly dumped a fry basket and refilled it. "I know you were looking forward to a day off. But if I had to spend the rest of my shift with him in here screaming at me, I'd have murdered him with a santoku knife."

"Lindsay!" a familiar bellow sounded.

"Hold that thought," Lindsay muttered. The chest-high

swinging doors that separated the kitchen from the dining area bounced open, and Bill Neldstrom's beefy frame filled them.

"You took your time getting here." The man's florid complexion looked ruddier than usual. Lindsay had long thought he was one tantrum away from a heart attack. "Take over the grill. Song has managed to burn every damn thing she's put on it waiting for you." The man's words had anger flushing Song's cheeks, although the woman kept her eyes downcast. "Place is full out there. Every mother's sister musta decided to do some Christmas shopping today." His words abruptly halted as he stared at Lindsay's face. "What the hell happened to you?"

It took a moment for Lindsay to follow his transition. Then she remembered her cheek. The cover-up she'd used hadn't done much to hide the bruise. "Walked into a door," she lied blandly.

He gave a short laugh. "Good one. Told ya that mouth of yours would get you in trouble someday." He abruptly shifted back to business. "See that you stay caught up in here. I don't want people bitching about waiting for their food. I'll try to come in and help out when I have time."

"You have enough to do out there," Lindsay told him, crossing to the order window to snatch a handful of tickets. "Song and I can handle the kitchen."

"Make sure you do."

The man was a bundle of charm. Turning, he exited the room again and Lindsay heard Song's audible sigh of relief.

"You always manage him better than the rest of us."

"Considering that I'm here on my day off, that isn't saying much." And considering that Bill Neldstrom was little more than a workplace bully, he was hardly a challenge. After consulting the tickets she'd grabbed, Lindsay said, "Can you handle the salads and the fryers?"

"Sure."

Lindsay placed the orders where both of them could see them and crossed to the walk in-freezer. "Heard there was some trouble this morning."

"Where'd you hear about that?" Song's voice sounded behind her. Without waiting for an answer, the other woman went on, "It was over-the-top, even for Bill. He dumped a full breakfast special on Mitch Engels and told him to never come back. Chang was furious. He had to fill the order all over again."

Selecting a couple of chicken breasts and a pound of bacon, Lindsay swiftly made her way back to the grill. Piper's breakfast menu was available until two, but lunch orders were filled all day. She couldn't imagine anyone wanting a chicken sandwich before ten in the morning, but her job was filling the orders, not offering nutritional advice. "I don't imagine Mitch was any too pleased about it, either," she said dryly, as she dropped the two chicken breasts on the grill.

A shrug sounded in Song's voice. "Well, he had been fired, after all. And he should have known there was no use coming back and appealing to Bill. It's not like he's ever going to change his mind."

Lindsay had told Mitch much the same thing last night, although the man obviously hadn't listened. For a moment she entertained the idea of dumping potatoes and gravy on Bill's slicked-back dark hair the day she turned in her resignation. The visual image was tempting. But timing was everything. She'd have to resign immediately after collecting her pay, or she could kiss her last payment goodbye. As Mitch had already discovered, Bill wasn't the forgiving sort.

A few hours later the breakfast rush had segued into the lunch crowd with no noticeable lag in between. Lindsay's cheek was throbbing, but she hadn't had time to take the pain reliever she'd tucked into her purse. For that matter, she hadn't had time to use the cell phone she'd slipped into her jeans pocket, either. She flicked a glance at the clock. Five hours until Jack was supposed to pick her up. She needed to make the call to cancel, and soon.

"What the hell?"

There was a crash behind her. Lindsay whirled, saw the broken dishes lying at Bobby's feet. The question on her lips died as she followed the direction of the boy's gaze.

"Everyone head into the dining area. Now."

Her brain seemed frozen. The voice belonged to Mitch Engels. But the man standing before her could have been a stranger. In faded camouflage fatigues and a bright orange hunting cap, he looked like Elmer Fudd ready to wage war on a flock of ducks.

But there was nothing comical about the shotgun strapped across his chest. Or the handgun he was holding.

"Mitch!"

His face, when he saw her, was as dismayed as Lindsay's voice had been. "I told you not to come here. I told you!"

She couldn't look away from the gun in his hand. It was still easy to recall the feel of a cold barrel pressed against her temple. Still all too easy to hear that voice in her ear, menacing. Amused.

Does this bullet have your name on it? Should we find out?

"Bill called me in for Chang," she said inanely. "Mitch…" She swallowed hard, tasted fear. "You don't want to do this. This isn't the way."

"It's the only way." With a jerk of his head, he told them, "All of you, into the dining area."

Lindsay looked at Song and Bobby. They seemed frozen in place, their gazes glued on the gun Mitch was wielding. She hesitated, a thousand scenarios fast-forwarding through her mind. There were three of them. If they all rushed him at once…or if she distracted him, would Song and Bobby react quickly enough to head for the exit?

But the other two workers were already moving to obey, leaving Lindsay remaining to face him. "You don't want to mess with me, Lindsay," Mitch warned. "You really don't. Out there with them. Now."

He blocked her path to the exit. She paused infinitesimally. A person knowledgeable about firearms was deadly. An armed person without that knowledge, even more so.

She turned, following closely behind Song and Bobby.

"What the hell are you doing out here?" She heard Neldstrom's voice. "Are you the one who dropped the dishes in the kitchen? Because I'm taking them out of your pay, you butter-fingered little freak. I'm not made of—" His voice broke off as Song and Lindsay appeared before him. "What's going on? Lindsay, you better not be staging a…"

Lindsay could tell the exact moment Neldstrom saw Mitch behind her. His eyes bulged and his face went a darker shade of red. "Engels, what do I have to do to keep you out of here?"

Mitch nudged Lindsay aside. "I think you've already done plenty, you spineless bastard."

The color abruptly leached from the owner's face when he saw the gun the man was holding. "Are you crazy? The place is full of people."

"I didn't come for them. I came for you."

Mitch swung the gun to aim for Neldstrom, who stumbled back several steps. A woman in the nearest booth spotted the weapon and let out a window-rattling shriek. Neldstrom took the opportunity to run for the door, slamming into Bobby and knocking him to the floor.

"You aren't going anywhere!" As Lindsay watched in horror, Mitch fired a shot, striking Neldstrom in the back. "I'm in charge here now! I'm in charge!"

Neldstrom dropped heavily to the floor, landing almost on top of Bobby. The teenager yelped, scrambling to his feet, his eyes dark pools of shock in his pale face. A baby wailed, women screamed and several patrons got to their feet and rushed for the exits.

Lindsay finally found her voice. "Mitch…"

"Everyone freeze!" Mitch raised the gun and fired two more shots in quick succession. The tableau inside the restaurant stilled, as if a movie had been paused midscene. "Bobby, lock the front door and close the shades on the windows. Now!"

The boy didn't move. "But…but…Bill…"

"He doesn't look like he's up to it," Mitch said callously. The owner hadn't moved. Blood was pooling between his shoulder blades. Mitch raised his voice. "Everyone sit back down. Go on. Get back in your booths. No one will get hurt if you do exactly as I say."

Lindsay studied him closely. The transformation that had come over the man was as fascinating as it was frightening. Gone was the cowed, victimized man from the bar last night. It was as if by donning that ridiculous hunter's uniform and picking up a weapon, he'd become someone she didn't know.

And that meant she wasn't at all sure how to approach him.

"Mitch." It took effort to keep her voice steady, her manner matter-of-fact. "Someone passing by is sure to report the shots fired in here." The location of the windows made it doubtful anyone had witnessed Bill's shooting. "You need to get away before the police come." She was hyperaware of the body lying motionless on the floor, of the blood seeping too rapidly from it. If she could convince Mitch that he was her primary concern, maybe they could avoid any more bloodshed.

"I'm not going without Alex," he said grimly, his eyes scanning the crowd as they returned to their seats. "Where is he?"

"I…I don't know," she answered truthfully. She hadn't been outside the kitchen since arriving this morning. "But you have to leave now, Mitch. You don't have much time." From the corner of her eye she could see that Bobby had secured the front door and rolled down the blinds to cover the bank of front windows

"Everyone keep your hands on the tables," Mitch called to the patrons. "And don't worry. The only ones dying today are the ones who deserve it. And if you don't do anything stupid…well, then you won't deserve to die, will you?"

"You could slip out the kitchen entrance the same way you came in," Lindsay told him, desperation tingeing her tone. Did the man intend a siege here? A sense of impending doom lodged in the pit of her belly. "If you leave now…"

Mitch reached out and grabbed Song, who seemed shell-shocked. Wrapping an arm around her throat, he told Lindsay, "Go lock the kitchen door. Then the back exit. I trust you, Lindsay. Don't screw me over." He placed the muzzle of the gun against the woman's temple, and panic filled her expression. "Or the next one that dies will be on your conscience."

Lindsay's gaze locked with Song's. The woman's eyes were wide with terror and a silent plea that was impossible to ignore. A kaleidoscope of possibilities raced through her mind, but in the end she knew there was only one choice.

Jerkily, she nodded. "All right. Don't hurt her. Mitch?" She waited for him to look at her. "Promise you won't hurt anyone else."

For a moment there was a flicker in his eyes and she saw the man she'd once thought she'd known. "I won't hurt Song. As long as you do what I say."

As Lindsay pushed through the swinging doors to the kitchen, it occurred to her that he hadn't exactly given the promise she'd asked for. Casting a look over her shoulder, she saw Mitch's attention fixed on her.

So she turned her gaze forward again and kept her movements stealthy as she reached under her apron on the way to the door. Pulled the cell phone from her jeans pocket. Sending a silent prayer to a frequently absent God, she rang Jack Langley's number.

"This is total bullshit!" Unable to remain silent any longer, Jack surged to his feet, paced Captain Telsom's office. "Fallon's threatening to bring charges against *me?*"

"You broke his nose and a couple of his ribs," Telsom reminded him from behind his scarred oak desk. "He's screaming brutality, which is going to bring IA breathing down our necks. You're sure we're solid on that attempted rape charge against him?"

"It's solid." Sheila Jennings had sworn out a complaint last night while Fallon had spent the night in the hospital. There was definitely something backassed about that turn of events. He hadn't had time to look at the report this morning, since he and his partner had been called out to check on an alleged burglary. After a couple hours at the scene, the elderly home owner had discovered his coin collection had been moved by his housekeeper. "And I'm not the one who broke his nose. That was the woman who

witnessed him trying to rape Sheila Jennings last night."
In short, succinct terms he relayed Lindsay's part in the
incident, ending with, "This is just a preemptive strike on
Fallon's part. He figures a complaint is going to be sworn
out against him and he's trying to keep his ass out of jail."

Some of the tension eased from Telsom's craggy face.
"Bradford's statement will back up Jennings's?"

Jack halted, folding his arms across his chest. "Yes,"
he said, with more certainty than he was feeling. His per-
suasive powers had been singularly ineffective with
Lindsay last night. But surely she'd be thinking more
clearly today.

"Then bring her in here and get the paperwork done.
Let's clean this up before it gets messy, Langley." His pro-
truding brow and deep-set eyes were even more noticeable
when he was wearing a scowl. "I don't like messes."

"I'll take care of it." Jack walked out of the office, glancing
at his watch. Three-ten. If he was going to get Lindsay in here
for a statement today, he didn't have much time.

When he got back to his desk and reached into his suit
jacket for his cell, however, he saw he'd already missed a
call from Lindsay. No message. Something inside him lightened. He knew better than to believe that she'd come to her
senses and rethought her decision about the statement. More
than likely she was calling to cancel their date tonight.

He pressed the redial button and held the cell to his ear,
sinking into his desk chair, a sense of anticipation clenching in his gut at the thought of speaking to her again.

But the phone merely rang, and rang, and rang before
switching to her voice mail.

Lindsay felt the phone vibrate in her apron pocket and
thanked God she'd thought to mute it before locking the

door and facing Mitch again. Because he wasn't the same man she'd felt sorry for last night. Something had snapped inside him and he'd spiraled rapidly out of control.

Like the rest of the people inside the restaurant, her attention was glued on the scene unfolding between Mitch and Alex Gardner, who had been discovered hiding below the order counter.

"I said crawl over here, you piece of crap!"

There was a shrill ring to Mitch's voice that had Lindsay considering him carefully. The unusual veneer of control he'd worn when he'd entered the kitchen was definitely thinning. She scanned the occupants of the restaurant, counting heads. Thirty-seven people, including the help. The customers were predominantly women, with five children and three men. And everyone wore similar expressions of dazed terror.

"Not laughing anymore, are you, funny guy?" Alex was on his knees in front of Mitch, his eyes squeezed tightly shut. Mitch had the revolver pressed against the center of his forehead. "What's the matter? This isn't as funny as watching Bill pour juice over my head? Something's wrong with your sense of humor, pal. This is funny as hell."

Alex's face crumpled. Silent tears ran down his face.

Lindsay sidled away until the hostess's lectern was between her and the two men. Leaning against the wall, she reached one hand into the wide front pocket of her apron, in search of the still-vibrating phone. If she could just open it, Jack would be able to hear everything going on, wouldn't he? And then maybe he could understand enough to send the help necessary to...

"Lindsay!"

Her heart stuttered to a stop in her chest, her fingers

releasing the phone and slipping out of the pocket again. Mitch was staring at her, frowning. "What?" With a sense of despair she realized the cell had ceased vibrating.

"Bring me a glass of orange juice. No, bring me a whole damn pitcher. Let's see how funny boy likes it when it's dumped over his head."

"He didn't do anything to you, Mitch." With effort, she kept her gaze off Alex and on the man holding the gun. She didn't know Gardner well, but he couldn't be more than twenty. About the same age as her friends were when they'd died. Had Wendy and Rick been forced to their knees just like Alex? Had Nathan been humiliated before the trigger had been pulled? She never would have thought that Mitch had anything in common with Niko Rassi.

But she'd never before considered what constant belittling and humiliation could do to a fragile ego.

"He laughed at me, didn't he?" Mitch's tone turned plaintive. "I told you that this morning. He watched Bill dump a breakfast special on me and the whole time he just stood…there…and smirked." He punctuated his final words by pressed the muzzle of the gun harder and harder into Alex's skin. "So get me that juice. He has this coming."

She swallowed hard. "No."

Mitch's eyes bugged as he stared at her. "I thought you were my friend! I thought you were on my side!"

"I am your friend." Lindsay had to force the words through a suddenly dry throat. It felt as though all eyes in the place had turned—accusingly—on her. "And as your friend, I'm saying you aren't someone who deliberately sets out to hurt others." She couldn't look at the body crumpled near the doorway. Not if she was going to appeal to Mitch's logic. "If you continue this, you'll be just like them. Is that what you want?"

He stared at her for a long instant, and for a moment she thought she saw the old Mitch in his eyes. Before they turned hard again.

"I'm not like them. I'm fair. And Alex has this coming. You know it, don't you, Alex?" The young man gave a jerky nod. "So bring me that orange juice."

Lindsay drew in a deep breath. It did nothing to dislodge the cold hard knot in her chest. Would humiliating Alex defuse Mitch's rage or escalate it? Taking a gamble, she shook her head. "I won't do it."

There seemed to be a collective gasp in the restaurant. From the corner of her eye, Lindsay could see Song gesturing wildly for her to follow Mitch's orders. But indulging this little power play he was on could only lead to increased violence.

The man's eyes widened. "Are you forgetting who has the gun, Lindsay?"

"You're in charge. I get that. But this is wrong and you know it."

Mitch's lower lip jutted out petulantly. Turning his focus from her he barked, "You! First booth on the left! Bring up your glass of milk."

And as Lindsay watched him order one customer after another to file up and pour the contents of their glasses over Alex's head, she surreptitiously dialed Jack's number again.

Jack was just finishing the report on the alleged burglary from this morning when his alphanumeric pager went off. In one smooth motion he grabbed it from his suit pocket and read the shorthand on the LED screen.

Shots fired—Gunman w/hostages—SWAT response—
1601 Lexington.

Lexington. The same call he'd heard on the patrol radio
minutes ago? Rising, he scooped up his jacket, and,
catching Lieutenant Coulson's eye, held up his beeper.
Coulson nodded. Jack headed for the door.

Lexington was around the corner and down the block.
He strode rapidly out of the precinct house and headed for
his department-issued Crown Victoria. Only three other
members of the squad came from his precinct. They'd
likely be among the first SWAT respondents on scene.

He jogged to the car, mentally mapping Lexington. It
was a street of businesses. A flower shop. A coffee place.
A couple restaurants. Some of the stores had apartments
over them. Could be a domestic call. No way of knowing
for sure until he got there. And not much use taking the
Vic when he was this close to the incident scene.

Popping the trunk, he swiftly unzipped his bag of gear and
donned the LBV vest with the heavy ceramic plates.
Securing the ballistic helmet, he reached for the 9 mm sub-
machine gun and double-checked that he had a full
magazine. He exchanged his department-issued secondary
weapon for the .45 Kimber and zipped up the gear bag again,
removing it from the trunk before slamming the lid shut.

Then he hefted the bag and ran to the corner. Turning
left, he immediately saw the crowd gathered at the end of
the street. Patrolmen had set up an outer perimeter and
were pushing the crowd back. As he drew closer he could
determine that Piper's was the incident scene.

There was a quick twist in his gut. He had a moment to
be grateful Lindsay wasn't working today before he

spotted the black RV that served as the tactical command post. Hitching the strap of his bag higher on his shoulder, he trotted toward it.

Ducking inside the command center, he saw the SWAT tactical commander, Harv Mendel, and a half dozen entry team members already assembled. The commander was midexplanation. "… differing reports, but there appears to be between twenty and thirty hostages inside. One gunman sighted. Three shots fired fifteen minutes ago."

"Any identity on the gunman yet?" Theo Basuk called out.

Jack's cell rang, and he gave a silent curse. He'd forgotten to mute it. Mendel sent him a narrowed glare as he cut it off midring and the man went on.

"Not yet. We'll station the precision marksmen on the rooftops surrounding the restaurant. The crisis negotiation team is en route. Let's get a laser monitor system set up right away. I want to hear what's going on in there. Run det cord under side one opening two to ready for a secondary entry distraction. All right, everybody, move!"

As the commander headed to the back of the RV, entry team leader Tom Nelson faced the rest of the members. "Langley and Basuk. Get us some ears in there. Hanks and Zook, grab the spool of det cord and let's set this thing up."

Jack moved to the back of the RV and took out the Pelican briefcase holding the laser monitoring system. Once he and Basuk were outside again, he said, "Rock, paper, scissors?" He already knew that the bayou-born Basuk would want the action part of the assignment for himself.

Basuk stared down his long nose at him. "First day back on the squad, Langley. You'd better take it easy."

Jack held out his fist. The other man hesitated, then cursed and did the same. A moment later, Jack was grinning. "Scissors cuts paper. Cover me."

Basuk uttered another oath and they headed toward the inner perimeter. "I'd say welcome back to Alpha Squad. 'Cept I'd be lying."

"That wounds me, Basuk. Deeply." Jack squatted beside his duffel and attached his radio and whisper mike. In his three-month absence from SWAT duty his spot had been filled. Which meant he was damn lucky a vacancy had appeared in the unit about the time he'd been cleared for the extra duty. "I was counting the days until I could work with you." He laughed at Basuk's retort, which was crude and anatomically impossible.

After discussing their approach, Jack donned elbow and knee pads before dropping to his belly, preparing to crawl up to the building to mount the laser transmitter on its tripod aimed at the front windows. The cell he'd jammed in his pants pocket dug into his leg. He pulled it out to shift it to his gear pouch, noting that the last caller had been Lindsay again. Dropping it into his gear pouch, he fastened the strap around his waist.

She must be real impatient to break their date. With the possibility of this incident stretching out for hours, she was probably going to get her wish.

Lindsay watched the clock on the wall. Time had slowed to a crawl. Mitch was still delighting in his torment of Alex. And her bright idea of calling Jack had gone nowhere. He wasn't picking up.

Which brought up the question of why the man had been the first person she'd thought of to call. The answer was troubling but it was the least of her worries at the moment. She'd gotten a free moment to place calls to Jolie and Dace, and she'd gotten the same lack of response.

A baby in the back booth began wailing, and nervously

she watched Mitch glare in that direction. She contemplated dialing 911. Just like calling Jack or her friends, she could keep the line open for the dispatcher to hear what was going on. But she didn't trust the dispatcher to catch on as quickly as she thought the others would. And she couldn't risk Mitch hearing a voice speaking at the other end of her cell.

Which left text messaging. If the police were outside, a SWAT squad would be called in, wouldn't it? And she recalled from the conversation last night it would be the one her friends and Jack served on. She knew Jolie and Dace didn't have the text messaging option on their phones. Did Jack? She'd never gotten particularly adept at the process but it was a way to send a silent message to him, and through him, to the police. And it would remain in his inbox until he was able to get to his phone.

Glancing at Mitch, she saw his attention had returned to Alex. But the ladies in the back corner booth, the ones with three small children with them, had their heads together, whispering.

Slowly Lindsay slipped her hand into her apron pocket, flipping the cell phone open. She couldn't do this blindly; she needed to sneak furtive peeks at the keypad. Her fingers felt thick, clumsy as she scrolled down to Jack's number before checking on Mitch again. She pressed in the commands for a new message and the blank screen blinked up at her.

"This is Dace Recker, with the Metro City police!" boomed a disembodied voice outside. "I'd like to talk to the person in charge in there."

"Oh, thank God," one woman sobbed. "Thank God."

"About damn time," Lindsay heard a man say.

"Shut up! Shut up!" Mitch screamed. His eyes wild, he looked around, fixing his stare on Lindsay. She stilled, certain for a moment that he could X-ray through the lectern to see her hand in her apron pocket. "It's the police. What do I do?"

The phone on the wall began to jangle. The baby wailed louder. A man began pounding on the window above his booth. "Get us out of here! This guy is crazy!"

Alex took advantage of Mitch's distraction and dove past him toward the kitchen.

As if in slow motion, Lindsay saw Mitch swing around, level his gun at the fleeing man and she grabbed the closest thing she could, a large, heavy, plastic-encased restaurant menu.

She heaved it at Mitch's gun hand, shouting "No, Mitch, don't!" just as the deafening sound of a shot split the air.

Chapter 4

Tactical Liaison Kurt Welter's voice sounded on Jack's radio. "From situation intel we know we've likely got one gunman. The owner is also verified inside. Running down the owners of the vehicles in the lot gives us at least thirty hostages. No identity of the gunman yet, although people are referring to him as Mitch. Doesn't appear to be a robbery gone wrong. Likely a customer or maybe a worker. The crisis negotiation team has been unable to establish contact. They're trying a throw phone."

Jack slanted a glance at Basuk, who stood silently next to him. "What about that last shot?" he muttered to the man. If they had reason to believe the HT was killing people inside, an assault would be unavoidable.

As if in answer to the question, Welter's voice went on. "From the reaction of those inside, however, it sounds like there's been no further injury. Exact position of the HT has not been determined. Precision marksmen have been unable to find a vantage point for gathering intel. Right now we're relying on the listening device."

Which, depending on the location of the gunman, could result in spotty accuracy. Jack turned to scan the area behind him. The outer perimeter was containing the usual crowd of rubberneckers and media. A couple news vans, cameras mounted on the roofs, were pressing as close as allowed. Any police action would be broadcast live to residents over their dinners this evening, increasing the pressure for a peaceful resolution.

He and Basuk stood ready with the majority of the entry team members at side one, the front of the restaurant. He thought of the restaurant blueprints they'd studied. A secondary entrance through the bank of windows could easily result in injuries to hostages, as booths lined the space beneath. At this point they had no way to know where the hostages were being kept. Their best chance would be to go in through side three opening one—the alley entrance— or side four.

The radio fell silent. Jack felt the cell phone in his gear bag vibrate. Surreptitiously, he unzipped the bag to withdraw the phone, intent on turning it off. He couldn't afford distractions, even though it looked like they'd be hunkered down for hours waiting for CNT to try and bring about a peaceful resolution.

He flipped open the phone, his thumb moving to the Off key when he glanced down and frowned. The LED screen announced that he had one text message from a number that was only vaguely familiar. Who the hell would be sending him a text message? Another press of a button elicited the answer—and had his blood turning to ice.

Insde Mitch Engels 2gun 1 ded advse

Abruptly, he reversed direction and raced back to the command center, ignoring the twinge in his thigh. His heart was jackhammering in his chest, and not just from the confirmation that they already had a fatality.

Lindsay was inside. She was one of the hostages.

"I'm not talking to them. Why should I?"

Mitch stood amidst the jumble of purses, cell phones and other personal belongings he'd had Song collect from the customers. After all, he'd explained to Lindsay earlier with a sort of eerie calmness, he couldn't chance one of them calling for help. She'd managed a sound of agreement through a throat that had gone abruptly dry.

What would Mitch do to her if he realized she'd done just that?

"You have to think about yourself. Getting out of here unhurt." Keep him calm. Keep him focused on his own well-being. That just might be their ticket out. Her earlier attempts to contact Jack had been useless, at any rate. He'd said last night that he'd be on the next incident call, but if by some chance there had been more than once incident response today, their friends' squad might not even be the one outside the restaurant.

Mitch looked unconvinced. "I've seen the movies. These guys on the phone...they're professionals. They just want to mess with my head."

"I think you can count on them to keep their word." She knew a little about the process from listening to Dace and Jolie, although she certainly wasn't going to share that with Mitch. "I'll bet there's media outside. There always is in a situation like this. The police can't afford to have something go wrong when the news will be broadcast all over. You hold the upper hand here, Mitch. But you can't use it if you don't talk to them."

"Oh, I can still use it," he said meaningfully, bringing the pistol up to aim at Alex again. Blood had soaked through the dish towel the boy had wrapped around his arm. Lindsay had managed to disrupt Mitch's aim, but her actions hadn't spared Alex completely.

"Try to focus." Because her voice was sharp, she made an effort to soften it. "Stop worrying about Alex and start thinking about getting yourself out safely."

"I'm gonna get screwed either way so it doesn't much matter what else goes on in here," Mitch said bitterly, his aim never wavering. "You know they'll pin Neldstrom's death on me."

Since he'd shot the man in cold blood, his logic was difficult to argue, but Lindsay gave it a try. "Not when they find out how he treated you, Mitch. There are laws against bullying. You can make them see that Bill's treatment of you drove you over the edge."

Finally his gaze left Alex and fixed on her, his myopic eyes widening behind the glasses. "They'll see it was his fault? That he had it coming?"

Lindsay could feel the condemnation shimmering off others within earshot, but she couldn't focus on what they thought. Only on what might get them all out of here alive. "But you have to make them see that. You have to pick up that throw phone they told you about, and—"

"No!" Abruptly his voice went fanatical again. "We aren't opening any doors."

"Answer the restaurant phone the next time they call, then," she went on seamlessly. "It's your only chance to tell your side."

"Tell my side," he muttered, but she could tell he was thinking about it. "I have to think."

Her phone vibrated inside the apron pocket and her knees suddenly threatened to give out. "Take your time," she suggested weakly. He wouldn't be able to see the slight movement of the phone, would he? "Why don't I get you something to drink?"

"Yeah, get me a root beer." Mitch kicked aside the jumble of belongings at his feet and dragged a chair from behind the hostess station to sink into.

Lindsay turned to go to the soda dispenser, reached for a cup to set in place. Then she shot another look at Mitch to make sure his attention was elsewhere before she dropped one hand into her apron pocket, flipped up the phone and read Jack's response.

"And this woman inside…you're sure you've got no relationship other than as witness to last night's assault?"

Jack answered the commander without a qualm. "Absolutely none." It wasn't a lie. Not quite. The kiss he and Lindsay had shared didn't change the fact that he barely knew the woman. The fact that he wanted to change that, wanted to know her on the most basic of levels, wasn't relevant here. Not when the admission would get him pulled from this duty.

"I gave her my number so she could contact me about that case." He lifted a shoulder beneath the heavy vest. "She knows I'm SWAT. She's a friend of some CNT members."

He withstood Mendel's steely gaze for a long moment. "All right." With an abrupt jerk of his shaved head, the other man seemed to come to a decision. "I want every message brought promptly to command center. You send nothing that hasn't been expressly okayed by me."

"Understood." He hadn't expected the commander to decide differently. With the snipers unable to gather intel, they had only what they could pick up through the laser. It was hard to ignore the best way they had to gather information about what was going on inside.

"Find out the number of hostages, positions, overall mood of the gunman. This Engels. And tell her not to do anything stupid. I want to see every message before you send it."

Jack nodded. He wasn't about to tell Mendel that he knew Lindsay well enough not to use any such phrasing. He concentrated on texting in the message, cursing his slowness. His fingers were too thick to make him quick at the process, which was why he rarely used it. He finished and showed the shorthand message to Mendel, who nodded, then pressed Send.

He turned, but didn't get back to position before he received a message in return.

37 hstg n wkrs mtch 6 ft insde fr dr tryn get hm answr phn. Call

Mendel grunted as he squinted at the text.

"Sounds like maybe she has him convinced to talk."

"I'll alert CNT. Ask her about the fatality. Anything the negotiators can learn before the call will help."

The commander strode away before Jack could point out the obvious. Which was just as well, because doing so would blow his claim that there was nothing personal between him and the woman inside.

Jack looked down at the cell in his hand, not making a

move to obey the commander. Because even if it hadn't occurred to Mendel, it had occurred to him.

Every time Lindsay answered one of the texts, she was risking her life.

"He *was* the boss from hell. You nailed it. Bastard was so cheap, he even took a cut of all of our tips. And he picked on me from day one. Anyone will tell you that."

Lindsay watched Mitch talk on the phone from the corner of her eye, misgivings circling in her stomach. She'd thought letting the man air his grievances to Dace and Jolie, the trained listeners outside, would be helpful. The long phone conversation offered her cover to send messages to Jack, but it seemed only to agitate Mitch further.

The baby in the back corner booth was screeching again. From his frequent glances in that direction, Lindsay could tell Mitch's nerves were fraying. Swiftly she finished her next message and pressed Send. And then, because she couldn't help herself, she took a moment to recheck Jack's last message.

Keep mtch clm hng in thr wel gt u all out. Prmse

His assertion that he'd get them all out safely might be empty, but it still brought Lindsay a momentary glow. And there was no denying that every message she got from Jack made her a little steadier. They weren't alone. That was something.

She scanned the people huddled at their booths and tables, voices muted. Her gaze lingered on the expressions of Song, Bobby and Alex. The inner glow faded. Because in here, they *were* alone.

She headed for Mitch. "These people will need to go to

the bathroom soon. And the kids probably need to go now," she said in a low undertone. Maybe she'd wasted her time texting while he was otherwise occupied. She could have slipped into the kitchen, searched for a weapon. She didn't like her chances with a knife against a gun, but she resolved to grab one if the opportunity presented itself. She'd feel better if she were armed.

"I'll have to think about it." Mitch's voice was distracted, and at first Lindsay couldn't tell whom the words were meant for. A few minutes later when he hung up, it became clear. His tone was icy when he told Lindsay. "No one moves. Those are my orders."

"You're making the decisions." Her words were as deferential as she could manage. "It's not going to smell too good in here after a while, though. I'm not sure how much longer these kids can hold it, are you?"

He sent the squalling kid in the corner a jaundiced glance. His voice dropped to an undertone, meant for her ears alone. "There are other ways to shut them up."

Fear pierced her. "No need to make hasty decisions, Mitch. You told them on the phone you had things to think over. That was the right thing to do."

"I told them what they wanted to hear. Bought time, that's all." He reached up with one camouflaged sleeve to wipe his glistening forehead beneath the orange cap, which was growing slightly wilted. His broad face was flushed. "As long as they think I might go out, they won't send cops rushing in here."

As long as they think I might go out...

She tried a smile but wasn't sure she pulled it off. "It will all be on your terms, Mitch. Take the time you need. You'll make the right decision. The safest one for you."

"I'm not stupid, Lindsay." His voice was so low she had

to strain to make out the whispered words. She heard the resignation in his voice. Saw the acceptance in his expression. "Even if I get out of here, then what? I can't go to prison. You saw the way Bill treated me. Think I'm not going to be a victim inside? I couldn't take that life. You're right about one thing, though. It will be on my terms. After today, I'll be remembered, all right. I'll make sure of that."

There was a roaring in her ears. Her heart sped up to triple time, until she was certain everyone around her could hear its mad beating. "There's always more than one solution. Talk to them again when they call. You'll see."

The child's crying intensified and in the next moment Mitch whirled around and screamed, "Shut that brat up!"

"You don't need this agitation," she said, inwardly quaking at what she was about to do. What she *had* to do. The negotiators had every reason to think that Mitch was going to come around. That with the next contact, or the one after that, they'd be able to convince him to surrender peacefully.

But the man wasn't as easily manipulated as they thought. And Lindsay knew their time inside was running out.

Dnt b foold mtch nt cmg out hell kil evry1

CNT liaison Herb Simpson, Kurt Welter and Commander Mendel took turns squinting at the text on the cell-phone screen. "Where are your negotiators with this guy?"

Simpson shook his head. "Still in the rapport-building stage. The HT hasn't escalated, but neither has he taken any positive steps like releasing a hostage."

"According to this text, he isn't going to," Welter put in. "He's stalling."

"Have you gotten anything from the laser system that

would indicate the HT's mood?" Jack asked. There was a knot of sick fear lodged deep in his belly, formed by Lindsay's last message.

"Enough to know he's volatile," Mendel said flatly. "And we probably aren't picking up everything with the background noise inside."

Seeming to reach a decision, the commander looked at Simpson. "We need time to get into position. Have CNT make contact again. Keep him on the line as long as possible. We'll want the diversion."

Jack's palms had gone curiously damp. When he took the cell phone Mendel handed him, it nearly slipped from his hands. Once the liaisons left, Mendel told him, "Text her back and tell her to sit tight. That we've got it covered out here."

Relief battled trepidation inside him. Because a breach on the restaurant didn't lessen the danger Lindsay was in. Just the opposite.

He keyed in a text message and held the phone up for the commander to read.

Gve it tme we hve thngs cvrd sit tite

Mendel gestured his okay and strode toward the RV. But Jack didn't send the message until he added a few more words.

Im gng to get u out of thre

"They'll stay calmer if they're comfortable. Calm means easier to manage," Lindsay argued. The muscles in her neck and shoulders were tense from fatigue and stress. "I can take them to the restroom in small groups. You trust me, Mitch. I've always been your friend. Let me help you."

The other man looked uncertain. "It's better to keep them in one spot. Where I can see all of them."

"I'll be watching them. And you have to answer that next phone call." He'd already let one go by unanswered. "You want to stay one step ahead of the cops outside, don't you? You have to make sure they think you're playing their game."

As if on cue, the phone on the wall jangled again. Mitch looked indecisively from it to her.

"Go ahead," Lindsay encouraged him. "I'll handle this for you."

"Just a few at a time. But don't try anything, Lindsay." She felt a chill skitter down her spine at the threat on Mitch's face, so incongruous settling on that normally placid expression. "We're both going to die, I'm not going to lie to you. But I could make it very painful if you screw me over."

"You can count on me, Mitch."

As she skirted Song, who was huddled on the floor, the woman whispered, "Why are you helping him?"

Lindsay looked over her shoulder to find Mitch still looking at her as he reached for the phone. Facing forward again, she murmured, "Be ready. And stay down."

"Lindsay, what are you—"

The rest of the woman's words were lost as Lindsay clapped her hands sharply and raised her voice over the murmur of the customers. "We're going to use the restroom. I'll call up booths one at a time. Those of you with children will be called first."

She kept her back to Mitch as she directed the customers, some of them openly sobbing, into an orderly line down the narrow hallway leading to the restrooms. Her shoulder blades itched, as if waiting for the bullet Mitch had promised. Luckily, he couldn't read her mind.

If he could, she'd already be dead.

The front and rear exits were out of the question. Mitch had a clear line of vision to both. But in that long, narrow hallway enclosing the restrooms was also a full swinging door on the opposite wall marked EMPLOYEES ONLY.

That door led to the kitchen.

Nerves tangled in her stomach. Her fingers were clumsy as she texted while the first two used the restroom.

Sndg kids out thru ktchn dr

The minutes stretched interminably without a response. Maybe Jack was right. Maybe they should wait. Would Mitch really have the nerve to shoot himself rather than surrendering to certain prison? Maybe not, she decided grimly, as the first mother and child came out of the restroom. Maybe he was planning on suicide by cop if a breach occurred. That didn't mean he wasn't going to take out as many of them as he could first.

With a hand on the customer's arm, she halted the progress of her and her little boy. He looked about four. From the looks of his tear-drenched eyes, he was the one who had been screaming earlier. "You'll have to go back to your booth," she said in a whisper to the thirtyish woman. "But I can get him out. Through here. There's an outside entrance." She looked at the nearest woman in line who was listening, her arms clutching her little girl protectively to her side.

Lindsay spoke rapidly. "You have to decide now and you have to act normal. Go back to your booths afterward. Pretend you have a child cuddled to your side. Don't do anything to give us away."

The second woman acted first. Eyes hard, she gave a grim nod and unwrapped her daughter's arms from around her knees. She crouched down, hands on her child's shoulders and gave her a little shake. "Quiet as a mouse. Like hide-and-seek, understand?" The girl nodded, eyes scared but solemn. Lindsay squatted to help the child take off her shoes, then got on all fours behind her. "Not a sound, but scoot as quick as you can, okay?" Then she pushed the door open, drew a deep breath.

She could hear the child's breathing, abnormally loud to her ears. Could feel her own heart pounding like a herd of stampeding cattle. On all fours, they were hidden by the counters, but there was about a five-foot clearing in front of the door where they'd be exposed. All Mitch had to do was turn to look over those chest-high swinging doors at the right time and he'd spot them. Even if he didn't look down, the outside door would be in his vision. He'd notice if the bolt was slid back. If the door was open.

And then both she and the girl would be dead.

She could feel her phone vibrate in her apron pocket. The sensation sent a quick quiver through her system. She withdrew the cell and flipped it open to read the message.

Rdy but b dam carefl?

She smiled shakily, dropped the phone back in her pocket. She assumed Jack had meant an exclamation mark, but the question mark embodied her emotions. Was she crazy for even trying this?

They were at the edge of the counter now. She could hear Mitch clearly. "I don't know. I'm not ready to trust anyone out there. I need more time."

The words sent a chill over her skin. He'd already told her what more time meant to him.

They were at the door. At their most vulnerable point. She reached up, moved the bolt back. Turned the knob.

The door swung open as if of its own volition. She got a glimpse of black-garbed, helmeted, armed men outside it, and instinctively clapped her hand over the girl's mouth before she could scream at the sight of the alien-looking creatures. She pushed the child into the waiting arms, felt a hand grasp hers. Her eyes met a familiar dark gaze.

Jack.

He squeezed her hand before backing away, easing the door shut again. But that touch, even through his gloves, was enough to give her the strength to turn again.

Fear a cold tangle in her chest, she risked a glance at Mitch as she dropped to her knees again. Found him still immersed in the conversation.

"It's been like this all my life, you know? No one respects me. No one listens to me."

With his backdrop of petty grievances filling her ears, Lindsay made a return trip to the restroom hallway. Took the boy this time, who wasn't nearly as quiet as the little girl had been, and delivered him safely to the door. This time when she returned to the hallway, she made a point of rounding the corner, making sure Mitch could hear her directing the women back to their seats and calling up the next group. Then she sent one more message before heading across the kitchen with the third one, a toddler she'd need to carry.

5 kid

The pacifier in the child's mouth would keep it quiet, she hoped. Each trip across the kitchen seemed longer. How long would Mitch talk? She imagined they'd try to keep him on the line but he'd hung up suddenly the other time and could again.

The fourth was an infant, and Lindsay's stomach

clenched at the mother's tears as she handed him over. Another slow, torturous journey across the kitchen, Mitch's voice ringing in her ears.

Her phone vibrated. She halted behind the counter to check the message.

Aftr 5th tke covr

A pool of cold fear congealed in her stomach. They'd mount an assault then. Probably through the door she'd opened for them. Which meant she had to hurry, because every moment that bolt was undone she was in danger of being discovered.

"Lindsay!"

She had to clutch the wall for support at the bellow. It took every ounce of effort she could summon to hand the fourth child back to his mother, step around the corner of the restroom hallway.

"Yes, Mitch?"

He had the phone covered, and a glare directed at her. "How much longer is this going to take?"

Nerves tap-danced along her spine. "I'll speed them up. When I get through here, I'll bring you another root beer, all right?"

Seeming mollified, he said, "Make it an orange this time," and resumed speaking into the phone.

Relief had her going boneless. And she was ashamed at the strength of will it took for her to round that corner again. To face that mother holding out her baby. To make yet another journey across the kitchen.

What the hell was taking so long?

Jack was used to the spike of adrenaline, those little bursts that kept instincts charged and quivering at the ready. But he knew his reaction couldn't be blamed totally on adrenaline.

It was knowing that every time Lindsay crawled across the floor, she was making herself a target.

He waited with the rest of the primary entry team, a little aside from the hostage recovery unit, who were taking charge of the children Lindsay released. Each kid was passed through the door to a member, who wrapped the child in an armored blanket and rushed to a nearby uniform.

Time seemed to have halted. He willed the door to open again. He stood behind Nelson, who'd enter first and head right. Jack would go left, with the rest of the team alternating direction to set up a sector of interlocking fire.

"Status," he muttered to Nelson.

"Contact still established."

His lungs eased only slightly. When he'd heard Lindsay's name bellowed a few minutes earlier, he'd thought for sure she'd been discovered.

Anxiety was still snapping through his veins, never a good reaction when he was on point. And the hell of it was, it wasn't the situation that elicited the response, it was the woman inside, putting herself in danger. How the hell did a female he'd only met hours ago call this kind of reaction from him? He didn't do emotion. Other than variations of the "Hey, it was a great time, see you later" variety.

And he damn sure wasn't used to a woman tying his guts up in knots by risking her life. Whether stupidly brave or just stupid, Lindsay's actions would ensure that any incidental injuries that might occur upon entry wouldn't involve kids. Hard to argue with that.

But it didn't mean he liked the situation any better.

The door inched outward and his muscles tensed as

Reagen took a baby from Lindsay's arms. His throat went dry as the door closed again.

One more. Just one.

He glanced down at his watch. It seemed to have stopped but he knew it was just his own reaction making it seem so.

His radio sounded, the volume purposefully turned down. "Entry team one, ready. Contact terminated."

A fist squeezing his chest, Jack awaited further orders. Surely Lindsay hadn't had time to start back with the fifth kid. Surely she'd abort the attempt. She could hear the conversation. She'd know Engels was off the phone—

"You no-good bitch! What'd I tell you about screwing me over?" The words were plainly heard through the door.

"Compromise! Compromise! Compromise!"

Jack didn't need the radio command. He was already moving. Nelson had the door open. Jack threw in a flash-bang grenade, hoping Lindsay had gotten the hell out of the way. Two sounds were heard in quick succession.

The second was the flashbang detonating.

The first was a gunshot.

He followed Nelson through the door, running in a crouched position through the haze from the grenade. He sensed rather than saw Basuk behind him. Knew the rear was brought up by three other members of the entry team.

The team spread out, but Jack and Nelson advanced on the partial doors. "Throw down your weapon. Now!"

His specialized goggles protected his eyes from the haze. They allowed him to see the man in camouflage, wearing a bright orange hunter's hat, holding a shotgun over the top of those doors, coughing.

"Throw down your weapon!"

When the shotgun barrel swung in his direction, Jack

didn't think twice. He hit the floor, firing in quick succession. He heard other shots coming from Nelson. Saw the gunman jerk, throw his arms wide. Slowly crumple.

Only then did he become aware of the other body on the floor, curled up around a small boy who was screaming for all he was worth.

And the steady stream of blood flowing out of the larger figure.

Lindsay.

Chapter 5

"Why can't I change the channel? Oprah's Christmas special is on."

The blonde's grating whine drew a long look from Niko Rassi that had the blood draining from her face. What had he been thinking when he hired her? Every time she spoke he wanted to strangle her.

Her tongue darted out to moisten her lips, and a sliver of memory surfaced. Of course. Her appeal *had* been her mouth. Just not for conversation.

"Because I'm watching the news. Stick around and maybe you'll learn something. Otherwise get your ass to work. The bar needs polishing before customers start coming in."

The woman—Chantelle? Chandrelle?—snuggled up to his side, one hand stroking his thigh. "I'd rather stay with you, baby."

He thrust his heavy crystal tumbler toward her. "Then go pour me another drink."

She rose to obey, giving an exaggerated sway to her hips as she crossed the room in case he was watching. But she'd already been forgotten. Niko picked up the remote and flicked it to another twenty-four-hour news station.

Didn't look like Carletti's body had surfaced yet. Or if it had, the fat bastard had earned less attention dead than he had alive. A satisfied smile crossing his lips, Niko stretched out on the chaise of his Italian leather sofa, remembering the hit with pleasure.

Another flawless job. Another hundred grand wired to his Caymen account. And another little memento for his collection. His world was damn near perfect.

The blonde leaned over him to deliver his drink, her perky plastic breasts spilling out of the skimpy cocktail uniform. Taking the tumbler, he looked past her through the wall of one-way glass that allowed him to survey his kingdom from his second-floor office.

Or at least the front for his kingdom.

The club was nearly empty now, but in a few more hours it would be pulsing with light, music, voices and excitement. Sex, or people in search of it. He'd built Kouples up from a glam bar to the hottest club scene in New York, and it hadn't been just his connection to the Portino family that had accomplished it. It was his smarts, his guts, his cunning behind its success.

There was satisfaction in knowing that. But it was his other occupation that gave him true pleasure. His lips curved as he tipped the glass of vodka to his lips.

Chandrelle saw the smile and suppressed a shudder. There was nothing warm about Niko Rassi, not even humor. He looked like the prince of darkness, sprawled out in slim black pants and a loose white silk shirt, with his thick dark hair combed straight back from his cruelly handsome face. Some of the other staff whispered that he *was* Satan himself, but they didn't whisper it too loud, or too often. It didn't pay to dis Niko. People who got him angry didn't last long around here.

But Chandrelle was smarter than most. She'd changed her hair color and her first name when she'd hit New York, hadn't she? Landed herself a receptionist job at that plastic surgeon's clinic. Done her best work after hours, on her knees, and earned herself a pair of double Ds that would take her further in life than that college diploma her ma had always preached about.

Niko put that aging, flabby surgeon to shame. He might be ruthless but he was rich and he was good-looking. If she played her cards right he'd spend some of that money on her one of these days. Especially if she became one of his favorites.

Mentally congratulating herself for coming in early, she sat down on the couch next to him, one hand slyly placed in his crotch. "You work too hard," she cooed, leaning toward him to kiss his neck. "I'll bet I can distract you from the boring old news."

Niko reared back, studied her narrowly. "I'll bet you can," he murmured. He shoved her head to his lap, stretching in anticipation as she unzipped his pants. With his free hand he picked up the remote and flipped to CNN.

Attention only half on the news, he recalled exactly why he'd hired the blonde. Everyone had a talent. She might be brainless, but she could suck the chrome off a trailer.

He wasn't focused on the story the anchor was reporting. It was the pictures flashing across the screen that had him straightening abruptly, the blonde and those limber lips forgotten.

"Hey! You gotta relax, baby."

But his attention was honed on the big-screen TV, disbelief raging through him. It couldn't be her. She'd dropped off the edge of the earth three years ago. He should know. He'd spent nearly that long searching for her.

But damn, it'd looked like Gracie. He grabbed the remote, turned up the volume.

"The incident left two dead and two others wounded. Ms. Bradford is credited with getting four children to safety before Metro City police shot and killed the gunman."

There! There was that face again, a camera shoved close to it as she was carried by on a stretcher. He stared hard, trying to see through the surface differences to the woman he'd known as Grace Feller.

Yeah, yeah, the yards of red hair were gone. Hair he'd loved wrapping around his hands while he pounded himself into her. She'd had it cut shoulder length and dyed a nondescript dark brown. Couldn't see the color of her eyes, but contacts could change them from that unbelievable grass-green, anyway. The shape of them was the same, though, wasn't it? And those kiss-my-ass cheekbones that made her look like a slumming princess instead of a dairymaid fresh off a Wisconsin farm.

The news went on to something else, and he flipped through the channels, trying to find the story featured on another station. No luck.

The blonde was taking his distraction personally, and applying all her considerable skill to coax his attention back to her. But the excitement firing through his blood couldn't be credited to her.

It wouldn't do to get his hopes up. He'd call Horatio, get a copy of that telecast first thing and go over it again. Blow up those shots of the woman and then they'd see.

Yeah, then they'd see.

He'd gone rock hard and the blonde gave a pleased little hum. He didn't bother to tell her that his reaction had nothing to do with her and everything to do with a woman named Grace Feller.

And the bullet he still carried with her name on it.

"Hospitals creep me out."

Lindsay cocked an ironic brow at Jolie, although the other woman wouldn't see it as she prowled around the room. "Really? I, on the other hand, love them."

Jolie stopped long enough to toss a quick grin over her shoulder. "Yeah, I know it's worse from where you're sitting. Or lying, as the case may be. It hasn't been so long since I was in your spot. I didn't much like it, either."

"Hopefully I won't be here much longer. Sorry you had to wait."

Jolie gave a shake of her bright blond head. "No big deal. I promised to give you a ride home and I still remember how long it took them to deliver my dismissal papers when I was here. I was chewing nails."

"I passed that stage hours ago." Lindsay was fully dressed in the fresh clothes Jolie had brought her. Her others were bloodstained and she'd be leaving them behind. She didn't want any reminders of those hours at the restaurant.

She wished she could leave the memories behind as easily.

That was what she got for ignoring the itchy feeling she'd had recently. The one that said it was time to move on, time to start over.

That was what she got for letting a broad chest and a crooked smile distract her from instinct. Maybe hormones grew more powerful with disuse, because hers sure had hazed her better judgment.

At that moment, the owner of said chest and smile stepped through the open doorway, a stethoscope draped around his neck. "Wanna play doctor, little girl?"

While Lindsay rolled her eyes, Jolie let out a disgusted snort. "Geez, Langley, could you get any sleazier?"

"I think we both know the answer to that."

Eyeing the stethoscope, Lindsay commented, "I hope the doctor you mugged to get that isn't the one I'm waiting for."

He skirted the question hidden in her words and studied her with an intent dark gaze. "You look pale. Are you sure you shouldn't stay a few more days?"

"Positive." If she'd had her way, she would have left after the first day. Two nights in the hospital were going to deplete most of her savings. And with Bill's death, she obviously wouldn't be getting her last paycheck. She didn't know what he had for family, but she couldn't bring herself to intrude on their grief to ask for money.

Which meant she'd be leaving town riding her thumb instead of a bus.

Trepidation pooled in her stomach. She had the hospital bill to settle. Then she'd have to spend her leftover money to change her appearance again, to get her hair professionally stripped and recolored. To find a place to stay until she had a new job in whatever state she ended up in.

There wouldn't be enough left over to buy new identification, at least not right away. She'd have to revert to one of her previous identities. That would be best, she decided, a slight frown on her brow. The Lindsay Bradford ID hadn't exactly been fraught with good fortune, and it wouldn't be smart anyway to use the same ID in two consecutive places. But still, she'd never resorted to using the same ID twice, and the thought of having to now filled her with unease.

"What's the matter?"

The concern in Jack's voice had her deliberately smoothing her brow. "Nothing. Just a headache." That was true enough. Even with the pain relievers there was a constant dull throb in her temples. She knew she was lucky it wasn't far worse. A couple inches to the left and Mitch's bullet would have been embedded in her skull instead of just grazing it.

She gave a quick shudder. And all these years she'd been on the run from Niko's gun. The irony was inescapable.

"Have you told the nurse?" Jack dropped the stethoscope on the bedside table and strode to the door, still speaking. "When's the last time someone checked on you, anyway? That's the way these places are. Won't leave you alone when you're trying to sleep, but come daylight you can throw a fastball down the hallway without hitting anyone."

"Settle," Jolie advised, shooting him an odd look. "Lindsay's fine. And the only nurse she needs is the one who's bringing the papers to spring her. What are you doing here, anyway? Seems like every time I visit her I'm tripping over you."

The words shocked Lindsay enough to have her attention arrowing on Jack, too. She'd thought she'd dreamed of him, his face floating above hers, tight with concern. His voice, filled with an unfamiliar softness. But she'd convinced herself it was just the product of a drug-induced haze, an embarrassing one at that. With everything she'd been through, why would this man be at the center of her subconscious?

Jack hunched his shoulders uncomfortably. "Just dropped by a few times on my way to or from work. To get an update."

His obvious embarrassment ignited her own. Or maybe it was the speculation in Jolie's gaze. Whatever, Lindsay was grateful when her friend was distracted by the short bursts of sound coming from her cell.

Jolie took out her phone, looked at the screen and frowned. "It's Trixie. I have to take this."

"Of course." Although Jolie was closemouthed about her biological mother, Lindsay knew the woman was dying of cancer. Despite the strain between them, Jolie was taking care of her in the last months of her life.

The other woman stepped out into the hall, her cell already pressed to her ear, braving the wrath of any medical personnel who might happen to see her. Cell phones weren't allowed on the floor.

Lindsay caught Jack's eye, and her throat abruptly dried. The intensity in his gaze was searing. "You did good in there." She had no difficulty following his train of thought back to the events in the restaurant. "Most people would have panicked, but you kept your head." His mouth crooked. "Even threw in some heroics for good measure. Pretty damn impressive."

There was that glow again, spreading through her chest at his words, even as the accompanying memory brought a shiver. "You obviously couldn't hear my knees knocking from outside. I was petrified the entire time."

He leaned against the doorjamb, arms folded and one booted foot crossed over the other. "All the hostages have been interviewed and the mothers of those kids are pretty grateful. You provided us our best intel with those texts of yours."

Lindsay rubbed her arms, suddenly chilled. "I understood what set Mitch off, but I couldn't change his mind about what he was going to do. No one could have. And that was the scariest part of the whole thing." Mitch Engels seemingly had nothing in common with Niko Rassi. Until she'd seen his implacable will, heard the unswerving determination in his voice. In the end, he'd been as intent on death as Rassi. And she was still trying to come to terms with that.

Jack's look grew quizzical. "You took a helluva risk. Kinda surprising for someone who claims to like playing things safe."

She could almost hear the sound of a trap clanging shut at his words. Because he was right. For all the care she'd taken with her current identity, that had been Grace Feller in the restaurant, not Lindsay Bradford. It was Grace who reacted without completely thinking through the consequences, to herself or to others. The recognition brought a quick little knife twist of pain. She'd become masterful at disguise. But she was beginning to doubt her ability to ever change her nature.

A nature that had brought her to Niko Rassi's attention all those years ago.

Because she was still the focus of that searing regard, she forced a light tone. "I surprise myself sometimes." That, at least, had never been untrue.

Jolie stepped back inside, her expression troubled. "No sign of those release papers yet?"

"What's the matter?" Because it was clear something was.

She ran a hand through her short tousled hair. "It's Trixie. She's being admitted. I'm sorry, Lindsay, I know I promised to give you a lift home, but I really have to get downstairs." Her smile seemed forced. "She can be a handful." Her words were rife with understatement.

"Of course you have to go." Lindsay waved her away. "Don't worry about me. I can grab a bus."

"Don't be ridiculous." Jolie was slipping her phone in her purse before she hitched the strap over her shoulder. "Jack may as well make himself useful. You'll get her home safely, won't you, Jack?"

Lindsay's stomach muscles jumped, then tightened at the expression in his dark eyes.

"Absolutely."

"This really isn't necessary."

"Hold still." Jack applied the ointment from the hospital with all the care of an artist applying finishing touches to his masterpiece. "You had to know that the dressing wasn't going to stay on in the shower. Are you sure you were supposed to get it wet?"

"I had to wash my hair," Lindsay said with a note of finality. The nurses had seemed curiously deaf to that logic, but there was no way she was going to spend another couple days with dried blood clumped in it.

She tried to peer past him into the small sack the nurse had sent along. "What else is in there for supplies?" Since she didn't intend to stick around long enough for the scheduled follow-up visit, she'd need to change the dressing herself, at least until the wound was healed enough to go without one.

One of his hands tipped her chin back into position, held it there. "You don't follow directions well."

He didn't know the half of it. But Lindsay sat meekly while he finished, until he withdrew a large gauze dressing from the sack. "Uh-uh, way too big. I just need something big enough to cover the injury."

"Bossy, too." His tone was amused, but he obeyed,

snipping the dressing in two before applying it and finally getting it secured to his satisfaction.

She cut short his admiration of his handiwork by pulling away and gingerly raking her hand through her hair to cover as much of the bandage as possible. She might have to hold off for a time before changing her hair color. The chemicals would be harsh against a barely healed wound. Maybe she'd invest in a wig instead.

Dropping her hand, she swiveled on her perch on the stool to face him. "Is the bandage showing?"

"A little." He reached out to bring a strand of her hair forward, his fingers lingering. "You won't be able to hide it altogether. It makes you look…sort of tragic."

As if embarrassed by the observation, and his action, he dropped his hand and busied himself putting the supplies neatly back in the bag.

She stared at him, stunned. "I'm not." The denial was automatic. It couldn't be termed *tragedy*, could it, when everything that had befallen her in the last three years was of her own doing? When every blessed consequence could be laid at her door, a dark divine justice for blithely doing just as she pleased six years ago?

Mitch Engels had been the first event in all that time that couldn't be blamed on her. The regret she'd carry from that incident at least wouldn't be tinged with guilt.

Jack scooped up the bits of wrapping and the soggy bandage he'd replaced and crossed to toss them in the trash. She watched him, admitting silently that he was going to be one more regret from her stay in Metro City, and how the heck had that happened? Jolie and Dace, yes. The friendship there had bloomed so slowly, formed so solidly, she'd had little defense against it.

But Jack… She'd had defenses raised from the moment

she'd first set eyes on him, for all the good they'd done her. For the first time in longer than she could recall she wanted a man. Not because she was lonely, or scared, but because of everything he was.

It was getting harder and harder to squelch that sly inner voice reminding her that she was leaving anyway. It would hurt no one if she indulged her desire just this once. And it was that kind of thinking, Lindsay told herself shakily, that made the man so dangerous.

Jack checked his watch. "Almost time for you to take a pill." Their trip back to her place had taken longer than it should have because he'd insisted on stopping at the pharmacy first, despite Lindsay's protests. She was too self-reliant for her own good, but without a car there was no easy way for her to fetch the medication later.

"That reminds me." She stood abruptly, steadied herself with a discreet hand to the counter when she swayed, just a little. "I owe you for the hospital bill. And the medication."

"You don't have to worry right now...." He was speaking to her back. She'd gone to the cupboard, where she withdrew one of those false soup cans that any thief worth his salt would recognize, and gave it a twist.

He eyed the bills folded inside it bemusedly. It had come as no surprise that Lindsay didn't have health insurance. Hell, millions of Americans were without it, and he'd already noted the sparseness of her belongings.

But when he realized she didn't have a checkbook, a debit or a credit card with which to pay, his interest had been piqued even further.

Because it would do him no good to do otherwise, he accepted the cash she thrust at him. "Don't trust banks?"

She busied herself connecting the two halves of the

false can and replacing it in the cupboard. "They're never open when you need them, are they?"

He weighed her words. There were people who didn't like banks. He'd run across a few.

He'd also come across people who needed to travel light and fast. Having to get money from a bank account would slow them down. He couldn't help wondering if Lindsay was one of them.

Since it would do no good to ask, he took his time placing the bills in his wallet. And wondered at the nerves shimmering off her.

She'd been calm as they'd dealt with the idiot at the Blue Lagoon. Shaky but determined as she risked her life in the kitchen at Piper's. But now that she was safely home in her apartment, she looked as jumpy as a turkey at Thanksgiving time.

Natural enough, maybe. He jammed his wallet into his back pocket. Anyone who'd recently had a bullet crease their skull was entitled to feel a little tense afterward. Most women he knew would be in hysterics by now.

Trouble was, Lindsay wasn't most women. It would be easier all around if she were.

She shut the cupboard door, then leaned against the counter, facing him. Other than the bandage he'd changed, which no amount of fussing was ever going to completely hide, she didn't look much the worse for wear. If she still had a headache, she was hiding it. Jack figured she had plenty of practice hiding all kinds of things. And it must be his occupation that made him want to strip her of all her secrets.

Okay. He jammed his hands in his pockets. *Stripped* might be a poor choice of words. And an impossible one to shake free of his mind, joined with that brief flash he'd gotten of her changing a few nights back. That memory had proven difficult to dislodge. Although there was nothing remotely sexy in the baggy flannel pants and loose T-shirt she'd donned after her recent shower, it was all too easy to recall what lay beneath them.

"So." He rocked back on his heels, trying to think of a blessed reason to stay. "You haven't eaten. I can call out for Chinese. Or grab a bucket of chicken."

Lindsay was already shaking her head. "I don't have much appetite. I'll get something later."

His gaze went to the cupboard door she'd closed behind her. "Soup?" The contents of the shelf had been bare of much else. He hadn't checked her refrigerator, but he was betting that would be sparsely stocked, as well.

"Probably. I eat—ate," she corrected herself, "a lot of my meals at Piper's. But I'm not really that hungry, anyway."

Too bad he couldn't say the same. Hunger, if that was the name for the heat firing through his veins, was about all he could think about right now. His reputation with women might be exaggerated on some counts, but not significantly so. Regardless, even he wasn't the type to make a move on a woman only hours out of her hospital bed.

"You probably need to rest." He meant to move toward the door. His legs just weren't taking orders from his brain yet. "Don't forget the information the nurse gave you. Keep up with the medication to stay ahead of the pain. Call the hospital if the headaches get worse or if the bleeding starts again and you can't—"

Her lips quirked. "I was there, too, remember?"

"Yeah, you were." Because he didn't trust his hands if he took them out of his pockets, he kept them tucked away. It took a supreme effort, but he finally got his feet to move. Unfortunately, in the wrong direction.

He took two long strides toward her, leaned in the rest of the way to lightly brush his lips across her forehead. "So make sure you follow the doctor's orders. You're not as tough as you think. No one is. If you need anything, give me a call."

It was just the right tone. Casual. Light. No sign of the knots coiling in his belly. Knots that tightened suddenly when her hands went to his waist. Lingered.

She tipped her face up to his, her green gaze steady. "You don't have to leave."

For a moment his mind blanked. It must have been his earlier sinful thoughts that had him painting her words with a deeper meaning. Could be it was just his nature to interpret things to suit himself. But a man could be forgiven for thinking that short quick glide of her palms up his waist a few inches, then back down, was more of a stroke. That the feminine fingers were curling, just slightly, into his flesh to convince him to stay.

Most of the time he'd have no difficulty testing just how accurate that impression was—and lingering to persuade even if his interpretation was flat-out wrong. But this wasn't most times. Lindsay wasn't most women.

It was a bitch to have to call on whatever better instincts he had, which he usually kept buried conveniently deep, to do the right thing. He should push her hands away. Remember she was hurt, shaken and probably not thinking clearly. Walk away while they both could look each other in the eye and head back to his place, alone.

He got as far as the first step. He covered her hands with his palms, but somehow forgot what he'd meant to do from there. Her next words managed to wipe his mind clean.

"I'm asking you not to go."

Chapter 6

A little thrill zipped through Lindsay at the shock in his expression. It was more appealing than it should have been to have a man like Jack Langley—who looked like he capably caught every pass life threw at him—fumble a bit when she issued the invitation.

And it was curiously arousing to watch his shock morph to hunger, to have the intense heat of it directed at her.

He didn't move but he loomed closer somehow. Didn't touch her, but she was crowded back against the counter just the same. "You're hours out of a hospital bed." The bitter regret in his words warmed something inside her. "I'm going to do the best thing for both of us and head home."

She would have been dismayed by his words if they were accompanied by action. But he remained motionless. Unless you counted the tension that seemed to radiate off him in waves.

She smiled, something easing inside her as she skated a palm up his chest. "You do that and your bad-boy reputation may never recover."

He caught her hand, held it fast against one firm pec. She could feel the rapid tattoo of his heartbeat beneath. "My reputation is solid. It can withstand the shock."

Heat transferred from his hand to hers. It surged through her system and had her bones taking on the consistency of warm wax. Or maybe that sensation was caused by the frustration she sensed beneath his words. Who would have thought to find chivalry beneath Jack Langley's tough, capable exterior?

"If this isn't what you want, by all means, go." Her hand curled, fingers entwining with his. "But don't leave out of some misguided need to 'protect' me. I have to admit, I've never been big on decisions others made for me. It's a weakness of mine." One she'd apparently never outgrown, despite the drastic consequences.

The skin seemed taut over his cheekbones. His mouth looked hard as he stared down at her with eyes as dark as sin. "Maybe I'm afraid you'll become a weakness of mine," he muttered. But she was encouraged when his mouth went to her throat, where the pulse was beating madly beneath the skin. "You need to take it easy, the doctor said."

Little flickers of desire spread through her muscles. She was helpless to stop it. "You're making this more complicated than it needs to be." Doubt niggled through her then, even as his mouth cruised up her throat, before getting sidetracked to the sensitive spot beneath her ear. Jack was the last man she ever would have expected complications from. But he had consistently surprised her since they'd met, with contradictory layers beneath that glib surface charm he wore like a mantle.

That alone should have had her inner alarm bells shrilling in warning. But they were muted by the thrill of his hands, sliding around her waist to pull her close. He widened his stance so that she was pressed against the V of his thighs. And the evidence of his interest was unmistakable.

His palm slipped inside her loose top, fingers tracing each individual vertebra of her spine as he smoothed his mouth along her jawline, nipped at her chin. His lips hovered above hers for a moment, long enough for their breath to mingle. Long enough for her to inhale his scent in greedy anticipation. And then his mouth came down on hers and the floor rocked a bit beneath her feet.

He packed a wallop, she thought dimly, senses drowning beneath the sensual onslaught. Need jittered inside her and her mouth returned the pressure of his, opening beneath his demand.

And that wanting didn't frighten her, not now. Because she wouldn't be here long enough for regrets to surface. She'd be gone before those complications could take shape.

If that thought brought a pang, it was also accompanied by a feeling of freedom. She could forget reservations and focus only on the hunger that was melting her system like overwarmed chocolate.

His tongue slicked along the surface of hers before flicking the sensitive roof of her mouth and drawing a shudder. The taste of him was simmering heat and dark promise. But she sensed restraint as well and wondered at it. Jack Langley wasn't a careful man. She knew that intuitively. He was wild and a little reckless, and she was honest enough to admit those qualities appealed. They mirrored her own.

She twined her arms around his neck and went on tiptoe, pressing her body more tightly against his, wondering just what it would take to slip the leash of his control. Her clothes hadn't been chosen with seduction in mind. The shower had wiped her face clean of the makeup Jolie had brought to the hospital along with her clothes.

If it weren't for the distinctive hardness prodding her belly, she'd believe he was disinterested. So it must be his misplaced concern that was holding him back. Keeping the demand in check and leaving her feeling slightly bereft.

And knowing he was the type of man who'd step back despite his own raging hormones revealed yet another layer, hinted at a depth she would have doubted the first time she met him.

Taking his bottom lip in her teeth, Lindsay scored it, not quite gently. A man like this could be dangerous, in more than the usual way. A man like this could be difficult to walk away from.

So she would run instead. The way she'd been running for the last thirty-eight months.

She eased back, opened her eyes, nearly lost her nerve. The control Jack was harnessing so tightly was visible in his expression. There was a primitive cast there, a grim resolve in his eyes that spoke of a man battling between nobility and emotion. To tip the scales, Lindsay grasped the bottom of her T-shirt and hauled it up over her head to drop it, forgotten, to the floor.

The leap of desire she saw on his face fanned her excitement and put to rest any lingering doubts she had about how this encounter would end. If Jack Langley was waging an inner war, nobility didn't appear to be winning.

His hands held an edge of roughness when he pulled her closer, and the evidence of his fraying control brought a jolt of sensual pleasure. "Chaste as a nun on the outside," he murmured, one long finger tracing the edge of the white lace bra where it skimmed the top of her breasts. "And all sorts of sexy surprises underneath." With his other hand he stroked the tiny hoop she had in her belly button. "Which is the real you, I wonder?"

His words had caution rearing belatedly, but it was dimmed when he hooked a finger in the elastic waist of her bottoms and tugged them down her hips. And the sudden savage hunger in his expression wiped her mind clean.

Jack leaned his forehead against hers for a moment, fought for control. She was a study in contrasts, the casual, careless attire covering lingerie fashioned to drive men wild. And somewhere in the recesses of his mind he realized the contrast was deliberate. He'd recognized she was a woman of secrets.

But the ones he wanted to bare right now were all too basic.

The scrap of matching lace panties were cut high on her sleek thighs, and he swept his hand up that satiny expanse to cup her bottom, to pull her more tightly against him. To hell with chivalry. It had never worn comfortably on him at any rate.

His mouth lowered to hers, all hint of gentleness gone. His kiss demanded more, and then more still. She wasn't a woman to give up her secrets readily, but he'd have no pretension between them now. In this area, at least, Lindsay would be totally honest. Emotionally. Physically.

His palm skated upward, fingers lingering on that spot on her shoulder blade where he'd find the tattoo he'd once gotten a glimpse of. He'd explore that, too. Along with every other exquisite inch of her. Places that made her sigh. Those that made her moan. He'd sample every soft and sleek spot of her and drive them both a little mad in the process.

He dispensed with the back latch of her bra with a twist of his fingers and drew a shuddering breath. He released her lips to lean back, as he dragged the straps down her arms.

And when the fabric peeled away to reveal the mounds of her high firm breasts, a hot fist of need clenched in his belly.

Her nipples were taut knots that begged for his lips. And the taste of her, when he bent his head to take one in his mouth, screamed through his system like a rocket.

He feasted on her, his free hand kneading her other breast while he sucked deeply from its twin. The little sounds coming from the back of her throat torched his passion, shredded any thought of going slow. As the sensations washed over him, taste and scent and sound, the world receded to hold only the two of them.

A woman like this could be addictive. One who could work her way into his system and have his blood chugging like a racehorse. She affected him with the speed and strength of a narcotic and was just as intoxicating.

Her fingers were unsteady on the buttons of his shirt, and masculine satisfaction flickered at the sign of her response. He lowered his hand and brushed the mound between her thighs, felt her jerk helplessly against him.

And then his shirt was unfastened and her hands were streaking over his chest, down his sides, on a tactile journey of discovery. Reluctantly, he released her nipple, but his hand never left her femininity, rubbing and circling gently until the fabric separating his fingers from her sleek softness dampened against his hand.

Her voice, when it came, sounded a bit frantic. "Take off your clothes." It was a demand, made more so by her attempts to tug his shirt from his shoulders, down his arms.

Nuzzling the base of her throat, he inhaled the scent there, and it sped to his pulse like a shot of tequila. "What's your hurry?" He kissed her then, all the demand coiling in his system impossible to hide, and gathered her closer so her nipples stabbed at his chest. And his hand continued to work her as his lips ate at her mouth in a frenzy of need.

He had a dim thought that a woman like Lindsay would seek to hold something back; she wouldn't give freely and she wouldn't give all. Mysteries deeply buried would be protected. But he'd have this. Every tremor, every shudder to her body. Each helpless moan and sigh. And he told himself that could be enough.

When he finally released her to step a few inches away, she used the small distance to rid him of the shirt. And then she seemed to go boneless when he dragged the panties down her legs and pressed his mouth to where she was wet, aching. Inviting.

Lindsay jerked against his mouth, unable to do anything other than feel. Mindlessly, her head lolled back, her fingers reached up to twine in Jack's hair to press him even closer. Her breath caught on a sob as his tongue tortured that taut bundle of nerves between her legs, and every ounce of strength leached from her limbs. Individual sensation careened and collided within her until all she could do was be and feel. And when he slipped one long finger inside her, she exploded into a thousand jagged shards of light.

She was faintly aware of the breath sawing in and out of his lungs, of being scooped off her feet and floated across the room. But then she felt the bed at her back, felt the mattress of the daybed sag beneath his weight. Excitement streamed through her again, a hard pull of renewed desire.

She rose to a sitting position and pressed herself against that broad expanse of back, the muscles sleekly jumping and working against her lips as he pulled off his boots. Sliding her hands down his arms, she curled her fingers testingly over the taut biceps, felt him quiver beneath her touch. She slid her palms over hot bare masculine skin, exploring hard angles and bone and sinew as pleasure quickened inside her.

When he turned, her hands were impatient, battling with his as she unfastened his pants. But when he dropped his hands, allowing her free rein, her touch slowed, grew teasing.

Hunger was already reigniting inside her, a thousand little pinpricks of pleasure humming to life again. But this time he'd join her in that intimate explosion. She'd demand his total surrender the same way he had demanded hers.

With excruciating slowness she worked the tab over the hard ridge of his arousal behind the zipper. She heard his strangled breath and risked a sly glance up at him. What she saw had the oxygen abruptly seeping from her lungs. His eyes were slitted. Sweat sheened his forehead. And the arousal on his face called a like emotion from her, flame leaping to meet flame until she shuddered with the longing to dive into that fire once more.

His hands took over for hers and shoved his jeans and briefs down, freeing his sex, which sprang forth, huge and hard and rigid. Lindsay took his length in both hands and lowered her mouth to lick the drop of pearly liquid from the tip. And when she took him in her mouth, his ragged groan torched something deep inside her.

His fingers were tight in her hair, her name a ragged groan on his lips. Until finally, with actions tight with tension, he freed himself and joined her on the bed.

A leap of wildness sprang forth at the expression on

Jack's face. Primal savage desire. And in this, she could be completely open. Completely honest. Because the ferocity of his hunger mirrored her own. And the evidence of it called forth every wild and reckless part of her that she had fought so hard and so long to suppress.

But she could indulge it now, with him. And the sensual freedom of that was heady.

With quick, desperate movements he sheathed himself with a condom. Then his mouth covered hers again, hot and urgent. His hands, when they skated over her, were just shy of rough.

The daybed shrank as Jack's large frame joined her on it. And when they pressed together, flesh to flesh, every nerve in her system flared to sharp, edgy life. Her neck arched beneath his questing mouth as he spread tiny stinging kisses along the sensitive chord there. And she realized, with a mournful tug from deep inside her, that this man was going to be far more difficult to walk away from than she'd led herself to believe.

Jack felt the change in her as her body melted against his, her touch slowing, as if she were a woman determined to sample a banquet destined to disappear. But the need inside him wouldn't allow him to slow. Wouldn't let her fade back from the sharp-edged precipice. He turned her over so he could trace that delicate butterfly with his lips as he kneaded the full, round globes of her bottom.

And he tasted. The sweet curve of her breast, the sleek slope of her arm. The narrow shoulders and surprisingly delicate vertebrae punctuating the long sleek back. Hands stroking and teasing, until she rolled to her side and her mouth to his, sealing her body against his.

Her hands as they raced over him were just shy of frantic. She touched him where he was hard and aching with deft, devastating strokes until he drew her hand away and loomed over her.

His blood was raging like a firestorm, embers of desire singeing him from the inside out. But still he lingered, even as his mind fogged and his vision hazed.

Nibbling at her breast, he sent a finger inside her, held it there, to savor the sexy little tremors that raced through her. And when he moved over her, slipped inside her with one smooth stroke, their moans mingled.

She was tight as a fist as she pulsed around him, and desire pounded through him, raging for release. Her legs climbed his waist, locking him to her in a gut-wrenchingly sexy prison. Jack stopped a moment to haul in a breath, struggling for his shredding restraint. But then she bucked beneath him, embedding him deeply inside her, and abruptly his control shattered.

He thrust into her, a wild, savage lunge, and she met the motion, increased the pace. Flesh slapped against flesh, and the frenetic ride to completion became the focus. His hands slipped under her butt to lift her, to seat himself inside her more fully.

Sensation chased sensation as their hips pistoned, bodies straining together. The sting of her nails, her short, harsh pants in his ear beckoned him like a siren's song.

He tried to drag his eyes open, to focus on her face, but everything was blurred as he lunged into her over and over again. He felt her crest beneath him, felt her inner walls milking him. Her orgasm signaled his own, and with one more wild lunge he followed her over the edge into a free fall of pleasure.

Her heart rate had slowed. Her breathing steadied. But the stillness of her form, still curled up against his side, was all nerves. Jack recognized it and knew better than to comment on it, so he did what he could to calm her. "Tell me something I don't know about you."

What the hell? Where had that come from? He frowned, shifting position, uncomfortable. He'd never had much patience for idle chatter after sex. Not when it was much more pleasurable to channel that energy into round two.

"That's wide open. You don't know anything about me."

"Not true." He settled her head more comfortably into the notch of his shoulder, skated a hand down her back and up again. Lingered on the tattoo on one smooth shoulder. "I know you had a misspent youth." She seemed to stop breathing for a moment. "Bet you ran off and got this tattoo and pierced your belly button to piss off your parents. Probably hooked school to do it, too."

He felt her lungs expand again. "You don't know as much as you think. I was done with school and no longer living at home when I got both." Her voice turned amused. "And you call yourself a detective."

Jack could feel the tension ease from her body at the light-hearted exchange. "Let's see what else my renowned deductive skills can come up with." His hand wandered over her hip, lingered on her inner thigh. "I know you're a natural redhead." She made a rude sound, and something lightened inside him. With the back of his hand, he brushed lightly at the auburn curls between her legs. "And I know you're traveling fast and light for a reason. Maybe it's a man. Maybe some other sort of trouble. But I could help. If you'd let me."

This time there was no mistaking her response. A chill chased over her skin. And noting it, he wasn't fooled by the light tone she managed. "Struck out again, Langley. But don't worry. I won't tell your captain you're losing your touch."

She pressed him back and settled herself on top of him, propped up on her forearms. "Since you're not doing so hot on your own, I'll tell you something you would never guess."

Something quickened in his chest. His arms came up to link around her waist. "Shoot."

"I'm a master whistler. Through my thumbs, both index fingers, thumb and forefinger… I can even whistle with my toes. Although you'll have to take my word for that one, because my mom convinced me when I was twelve that it wasn't ladylike."

"Maybe not, but it's definitely intriguing." Ridiculous to feel let down by her revelation. And stupid to admit he'd been waiting for something more. Something she'd give freely that had nothing to do with desire, and everything to do with a modicum of trust.

And that was just humiliating. If he didn't watch himself he'd be turning into a damn woman with all these notions of sharing, and then where the hell would he be? Well, on his back, actually, because if he were a woman he'd have sex *all* the time, just because he could, but that wasn't the point. The point was Lindsay didn't trust him. Not enough to tell him whatever the hell she was running from. And though everything inside him wanted to push, he held back. He'd conducted enough interviews to know when confidences couldn't be rushed. You coaxed the secrets out, built up rapport. It'd obviously take more time to do the same with Lindsay.

"How about you? Any hidden talents you want to brag about?"

"If you still have to ask…" He jumped a little when she plucked at his chest hair, a little harder than necessary. He'd forgotten about that mean streak of hers. "All right, hold on." In the interest of self-preservation, he covered her hands with one of his. "We'd have been a pair at twelve because I believe it was about that time I'd perfected the art of belching the entire chorus of 'Happy Birthday.'"

A helpless laugh escaped her, and he smiled. "Since I don't want you to think I was completely without charm, I'd like to add that two years later my claim to fame was being named most valuable player when I competed in the junior hockey league."

"Hockey?" She eyed him suspiciously. "In California?"

He shifted, settling her more comfortably. Maybe this talking after sex thing wasn't so bad. He did, after all, have Lindsay stretched out on top of him. Naked. "We have indoor rinks here, too. Got a full ride later to USC. I was good at skating and I liked to knock people down. Seemed like a calling."

"Hockey." She sounded bemused and he was oddly pleased that he'd managed to surprise her.

"Speaking of claims to fame." He leaned forward to nip her bottom lip, not quite gently. "I'm sort of surprised you haven't had reporters camped out on your doorstep already. I doubt you can count on that luck holding. You might want to hang out at Jolie and Dace's for a while. Unless I can convince you to stay at my place. My motives, of course, would be completely pure."

That stillness came over her again. He could feel the tension shooting into her muscles. "Reporters?"

Smoothing her hair back from her face, he studied her without seeming to. "You're the woman of the hour. Those heroics of yours? Splashed all over the media. Radio, TV, newspapers." He'd chased more than one reporter away from her hospital room that first night, before having a little talk with the hospital security. Must've done some good, because apparently her address hadn't been leaked yet.

"Well." Her smile looked forced. "A celebrity doesn't stay famous long, even in Metro City."

"Not just in Metro City," he reminded her. Didn't the woman ever turn on a TV? "You made CNN. The story ran national."

Lindsay felt her organs turn to ice, one by one. Glaciers bumped through her veins. A freight train ran through her chest, roared through her ears. Jack's voice seemed to come from a distance.

"I'm not going to lie. The pictures weren't the most flattering. But you looked suitably heroic. Wouldn't be surprised to hear the mayor was planning a ceremony in your honor."

National news. The words drumrolled in her head. And pictures. Of course there would be pictures. Now she remembered the flash of bulbs as they carried the stretcher to the ambulance. And it would all end up on the Internet. The cold radiated from her insides out. Jack felt it, tugged the sheet up over her. But his efforts were in vain. In that moment, she doubted she'd ever be warm again.

No reason to panic, she told herself a little wildly. What were the chances Niko would see that particular broadcast, even if it were on the national news? And if he had, what was the likelihood that he'd recognize her? She'd been careful. Her hair was shorter, colored. A different style. And though she hadn't used colored contacts for this identity, he'd never be able to determine eye color from a newscast. Her picture would have flashed on the screen for only a few seconds. He'd have no reason to look further into the story.

Although all true, the thoughts did little to chase the chill away. She'd ignored her instincts when they first began to warn her it was time to move on. But she couldn't afford to ignore them any longer.

"You know that food you were talking about earlier?" She hoped her voice sounded normal. Because her smile felt forced. "All of a sudden I'm ravenous."

He was silent a beat too long. "You want me to heat up some soup?"

"I was thinking Thai. Ming's is over on—"

"I know where Ming's is."

She rolled off Jack, avoiding his gaze. And felt far worse than she'd expected to for lying to him. "They don't deliver, though. Maybe we should call for pizza instead." She held her breath.

"No problem. I can go pick it up and be back in forty minutes."

Jack sat up and swung his legs over the bed, then rose, unabashedly nude. Lindsay wrapped the sheet around herself, too miserable to enjoy the view. The thought of sneaking away like a thief in the night seemed low, but spending even another hour in Metro City under the circumstances was too dangerous even to contemplate.

And that, she thought bitterly, was what she got for lowering her guard, ignoring her better judgment. For reaching out and taking what she wanted, even for a few hours. Experience should have taught her that everything came with a price.

Jack had his jeans on, was buttoning his shirt. "What do you want?" When she looked at him blankly, he elaborated, "From Ming's. What should I get you?"

There was a vise in her chest, squeezing the breath from her lungs. "I don't care. Surprise me."

He nodded. "I'll do that."

She watched him move to the door, walk through it. And then stared at the closed portal as if it held solutions for a problem she'd spent three years running from.

Hauling in a shaky breath, she swiped a hand across her burning eyes. There was only one solution to be had, and if she wanted to stay alive, she had to get moving. But it was peculiarly difficult to haul herself out of bed and head toward her closet.

Moving like an automaton, she pulled on clothes and shoved her gun and money into the bottom of her purse. After a moment she also threw in the bags containing the prescriptions and medical supplies. Then she dragged out her duffel bag and tossed the remainder of her meager belongings into it.

It took all of ten minutes to pack everything she owned. And that, in and of itself, was some sort of commentary on her life. But it wasn't one she wanted to spend time examining at the moment. She looked around the apartment, checking for anything she might have forgotten.

There was a jagged pain in her chest at the thought of leaving without a word to Jolie and Dace. She'd use a pay phone to contact Jolie, she vowed, on her way to wherever she was going. This was the reason she'd always avoided ties. They just made it more difficult—painful—when it was time to go. There was a weight in her heart, slowing her movements. Lining her stomach with lead.

She pulled the key to the apartment off her key ring, laid it on the counter, and forced her mind back to the matter at hand. Her rent was paid up until the end of the month. She'd repaid Jack for the hospital bill and prescriptions.

Jack. Nerves jittered. He'd be back in twenty or thirty minutes. She needed to hurry. If she left now she could catch a bus and get off near the interstate. And then she'd try her luck heading south.

Her feet began moving, ahead of her will. She'd never been to the southwest. Maybe she'd lose herself in Tucson or Phoenix. She pulled open the door, a flare of urgency urging her faster. Hurrying down the steps, it occurred to her that she should have taken another pain reliever. Her headache, miraculously absent while in bed with Jack, had raged back stronger than ever. She rounded the corner of the garage, intent on taking the sidewalk to the bus stop.

And ran full tilt into a rock-solid chest.

Two hard hands came up to steady her, failed to release her. Her mouth opened as she stared up at his face, but no sound came out.

Jack's smile held grim satisfaction, with an edge of mean. "Surprised yet?"

Chapter 7

Lindsay stared at Jack, shock dulling comprehension. "I wasn't expecting you back so soon," she blurted.

One black brow winged up in derision. "Obviously."

Reason filtered in belatedly and she tried to tug free. He still didn't let go of her arms. "I thought... While you were gone I figured I'd drop off a bag of stuff I promised to Dora Jenkins. My landlord," she improvised rapidly. "She's taking a load of Christmas donations to Goodwill."

He eyed her bag. "Now that's interesting. Because lousy detective that I am, I figured you were running out on me. I'd also hazard a guess that the bag is full of every blessed thing you had in that apartment." There was a little smile playing around the corners of his mouth that owed nothing to amusement. "Should we see how far off base I am?" He released her to reach for the bag.

Lindsay tightened her grip on it. And for the first time

noticed that his hands were empty. "You never went to Ming's!" So her outrage was hypocritical. There was an urgency building that made niceties a luxury. He'd obviously been to his car, because he was wearing his gun and shoulder harness. But he'd also obviously not gotten farther than that.

"Because your sudden *hunger* didn't appear until after I'd told you about the publicity." With hard hands he forcibly turned her and gave her a little nudge in the direction of her apartment. She tried to stand her ground, but she was no match for him when he placed an implacable palm at the base of her back and propelled her forward.

"So I thought I'd stick around a few minutes," he continued, voice terse. "Actually started to think I'd over-reacted. Been too suspicious. But here you are, hurrying toward the bus stop like your ass is on fire. So you'll have to excuse me if I'm not inclined to believe it's due to a sudden burst of generosity. Although I know from recent experience just how *generous* you can be."

That earned him a hard elbow jab to the gut, which, if he hadn't been crowding her so closely, wouldn't have hit its mark. As it was, he made a satisfying sound of pain, but it didn't slow him appreciably.

"Stop pushing me around," she ordered, seething. When they got to the stairs he grabbed one of her arms and practically hauled her up the steps, which only infuriated her further. "I said—"

"Yeah, I know what you said. It's what you *didn't* say that I'm interested in. So you're not going anywhere until you tell me what the hell has you so spooked. Who you're running from." They were on the landing now, outside her apartment. But when he guided her toward the door, she managed to break free and dodge around him. Only to be caught, when he turned, between the railing and a wall of pulsing angry male.

"It's none of your business—" she began.

He shoved his face close to hers, his dark eyes shooting enough sparks to singe her with his fury. "The hell with that. I'm not going to stand here and debate it with you. It *is* my business. We're connected, you and me, no matter how much you want to deny it."

She desperately wanted to. But the denial when it came to her lips refused to be uttered. She could only stare at him, a wistful sort of sadness twisting inside her. Because it had been a long time since she'd wanted to be tied to any man. And despite her better judgment, Jack Langley had called out long-dormant feelings in her from the first.

His expression, fixed on hers, softened marginally. "You're in trouble. Think I can't see that? But you have to trust someone, sometime. I think that someone should be me." He reached up to cup her face in his palm. "Now."

One of her hands rose to cover his as she fought the surge of longing that swept through her. How did he do that? she wondered wildly. How could he so deftly smash through logic and good sense to elicit a response based solely on emotion? Give the man another few minutes and he'd have her spilling everything, and that would put her in all-too-familiar territory.

A cop had been told the story once before. Disaster had followed.

Swallowing, she battled to wall off feeling, fought to summon reason. "I can't do that. It's not your—"

She felt the wood splinter near her hand at the same time she heard the muffled shot. Jack shoved her down behind him and drew his gun, crouching in front of her. "Get inside," he shouted.

The second shot sounded and he didn't have to tell her again. She'd left the door unlocked, and she practically dove inside, landing on her knees with enough force to snap her head back, increasing the hammering in her temples.

But when Jack didn't follow her moments later, she crawled to the still-open door. "Get in here!"

He tossed her a quick glance. "Use your cell to call 911. Give them the address and tell them there's an officer in need of backup. Go!"

"What are you doing?"

Jack continued down the stairs, his back against the wall of the apartment, gun ready. He shouldn't have been surprised that Lindsay failed to immediately follow his order. But at least she was no longer in the line of fire.

Because given the circumstances, with someone shooting at them, it was almost certain that she was the target.

Jack scanned his surroundings as he moved. The shooter was hidden somewhere in the backyard separating the garage and the main house. From the direction of the bullets, the gunman would have had to be hidden at an angle to the landing of the stairs.

The adjoining yard was heavily landscaped, with a man-made goldfish pond, complete with arched bridge. A multi-level deck covered the back of the house, leading down to a barbecue pit. The mass of green lawn was punctuated with carefully tended clumps of flowering shrubs.

But it was toward the gazebo in the center of the yard that Jack headed now, taking cover where he could along the way. Whoever had fired at them had to be close. That hadn't been a rifle. It had been a revolver fitted with a suppressor, from the sounds of it. Most likely a .45 semiautomatic. It wouldn't be particularly accurate from a distance.

He stopped behind a large boulder and studied the partially open building across the yard. He hadn't seen anyone running from the area, which meant the shooter was likely still around. Jack took an instant to throw a glance over his shoulder. Lindsay had shut the door, he noted with relief. She was safe for the moment.

Considering his options, he decided to try circling around the far side of the gazebo. It was longer, but going the other way would take him across the deck. If the shooter was still out there, a shot fired in his direction could hit the house.

He ran in a crouch toward a nearby thatch of low-lying shrubs, taking a flying dive when the next shots were fired. Hitting the ground heavily with his shoulder, he rolled, rose to his knees. A figure in black was racing across the yard and Jack's finger began squeezing the trigger.

Out of the corner of his eye he saw movement. Turning, he observed the elderly lady leaning to peer out of the back door of the main house. "Get inside," he shouted, his finger easing on the trigger. She closed the door, but remained framed in its window.

Jack cursed, rose and started racing after the fleeing figure. The houses in the area were pricey, each surrounded by an acre of yard. The man—and he was fairly certain it was a man—veered toward a ten-foot brick privacy fence and scrambled up a rope ladder dangling on the side. Long before Jack reached it, the ladder had been yanked over the top.

He came to a halt in front of the fence, breath heaving, and took a moment to scan the area. No way to tell if the gunman would cut across the private yard and over the other side of the fence or go out the front. Weighing the odds, Jack raced toward the front of the house, looked up and down the street. Seeing nothing out of the ordinary, he ran around to the other side, but there was no one in sight.

The old wound in his thigh was screaming, and there was a hitch in his gait when he jogged up to the front door of the huge stone house. He wanted a look in its backyard, but there was a growing certainty in his gut.

The gunman had already gotten away.

"You poor thing," Dora Jenkins crooned, pushing a large mug of fresh, steaming coffee into Lindsay's hand. "Drink this. You need your strength."

Maybe it was adrenaline crash, or it could have been the shot of vodka Dora had laced the last mug with, but Lindsay's head was swimming. Come to think of it, it might be the alcohol combined with the pain reliever she'd taken earlier. In any case, another mug was going to knock her on her butt.

Then again, the expression on Jack's face when he and the cop he was talking to glanced her way warned her that she was going to need fortification. She accepted the mug, sent a wan smile to Dora. "Thanks." Her fingers wrapped around the cup, seeking the heat transference. Her insides were infused with ice.

"I couldn't believe my eyes when I saw those men running across my yard with guns drawn," prattled Dora. She was a small, plump woman with a head full of gray pin curls, circa the 1940s. They danced and shook with her words, as Dora Jenkins did everything with a flourish, even speaking. *Especially* speaking. "It was just like something out of the movies. Especially that one… What was the name? Cary Grant was a detective. Or was it Gary Cooper? No, I really think it was Cary Grant, because I saw it with my husband, when we…"

Lindsay tuned out, trying to compose her thoughts, which were chasing around her mind like a cat after a mouse. It could be coincidence. An inner voice jeered at that, but she clung stubbornly to the idea. Maybe Jack had enemies. Or maybe the guy they'd stopped in the Blue Lagoon a few nights ago was angry about the charges filed against him. She'd broken down and written out a statement while she'd waited with Jolie to be dismissed from the hospital.

The thoughts continued to swirl, but there was a cold spear of certainty lodged in her middle. Because there was only one person likely to shoot at her.

Niko Rassi.

Bile filled her throat and she clutched the mug tighter. He would have had to move fast. How long ago had that newscast gone national? Yesterday? The day before? He would have had to act immediately, travel over two thousand miles in less than forty-eight hours. Was that even possible? Paranoia and logic battled. She couldn't be sure.

Her attention was diverted by something Dora said. "I'm going to go right home and take inventory. Martha Grimes's home was robbed just last month. And Sid Balkey said just yesterday that he'd seen strange cars driving up and down the street lately. Casing the places, that what I think. Why, how do I know he hadn't already been in my house? Could have killed me in the middle of my afternoon Pilates."

"You... There've been robberies on the street?" Lindsay's brain felt sluggish, but she seized on the information like a starving hound on a bone.

"That's what I've been saying." Dora patted her shoulder again. "You're overwrought. I don't blame you for being a little out of it. Why, if you didn't happen to have that police detective at your place, there's no telling what shape we'd all be in right now."

Lindsay huddled closer to the railing of the stairway, where she was seated on the bottom step. "No telling," she murmured.

Interest sharpening in her voice, the older lady's expression turned shrewd. "Just what was that police detective doing here, dear?"

Over the woman's shoulder, Lindsay saw Jack headed her way, and took a quick gulp from her mug for fortification. "He...ah...needed to go over my statement. From before."

"Of course." But the elderly woman's look that passed between Lindsay and Jack as he approached remained speculative.

"Ms. Jenkins." Jack's tone was professional. "Detective Paulson will take your statement." He pointed to the man he'd been speaking to earlier, who was standing at the curb.

Dora straightened, beaming, and fluffed her hair, her earlier curiosity forgotten. "My statement. How exciting. Maybe he'll help me take inventory at my house, too." She hurried toward the driveway.

Lindsay saw the puzzlement on Jack's expression and explained, "Dora says there have been some burglaries on this street. She's convinced this was a casing gone wrong."

He propped his foot on the step beside her, leaned in. "That's one idea."

The proximity, coupled by the frenzy of her thoughts, had her nerves skittering, tumbling one over the other. She took another swallow, although alcohol right now was probably not a good idea. She needed all her wits about her for this conversation.

And to plan how she was going to slip away from all the attention and get out of town, without leaving a trace.

"You okay?"

The husky timbre of his voice, the note that hadn't been there when he'd addressed Dora, added another degree of weakness to her muscles. "I'm fine."

He accepted the lie for what it was and lifted his head to look around the area. "I can't say that I share Ms. Jenkins's opinion, though. Unusual for a burglar to come armed, in daylight. Especially unusual to fire, other than in self-defense. It's not like we were a threat. Never even saw the bastard before the shooting began."

She gripped the mug almost tightly enough to crush the pottery and strove for an even tone. "I've been thinking that it might have something to do with the restaurant shooting. Maybe Mitch had a brother, or family members upset about the way it ended."

"And decided to take it out on you?"

It sounded thin, even to her own ears, but it was the best she could come up with, given the fact her focus was splintered into a thousand fragments. "Some of the witnesses at Piper's got the idea I was cooperating with Mitch. And he wasn't exactly singing my praises before you…before he…" He'd spent his last moments, she recalled now, her stomach sinking even further, cursing her fluently and imaginatively. She could have told him he was wasting his breath. She'd been living under a curse for the last several years.

"It's a thought." His voice was mild. Which should have warned her. He reached into his pocket and withdrew a clear plastic evidence bag. "Doesn't explain this, though."

He held the shell between thumb and forefinger and Lindsay stared dumbly at it. Read the engraving on the side. The engraving she'd known would be there.

"Any idea who 'Gracie' is?"

It was like staring into the headlights of an oncoming train. Knowing it was bearing down on her didn't lessen the impact. She couldn't respond. The simple act of drawing breath into her lungs was beyond her. Panic careened through her system, sprinted up her spine.

Somehow, she managed to shake her head. But she couldn't manage words. Not yet.

The last time she'd seen that shell, or its twin, she'd had Niko's hand wrapped around her throat.

See this? If you don't tell me where it is, this one has your name on it. Are you listening to me, Gracie?

She'd listened. And she'd managed, somehow, to convince him of her ignorance. Until she had the chance to get away. And kept running so the bullet encased in that shell wouldn't find its mark.

Caught in the past, her lungs ached for oxygen. She released the pent-up breath in a long rush, one hand going unconsciously to her throat.

"Somehow I thought you'd say that." He hooked a hand under one of her arms and hauled her to her feet, not ungently. "C'mon." He picked up her bag with his free hand.

She clung to the railing. "Where?"

"Downtown. You need to give a statement about what happened today, and then you're going to start answering a few questions. With the truth, preferably." His arm around her shoulders was much-needed support, but it also served to move her forward. "Although it doesn't seem as though you and *truth* are on a first-name basis."

That shot her spine with steel, for all the good it did her. He was still forcing her rapidly toward his car, and after a quick look around, she admitted that she couldn't stay here, anyway. Nor could she come back. Niko knew where she lived. That fact pounded in her brain. He could be somewhere around right now. Watching. Waiting.

Her throat went dry at the thought, and she forced herself to focus. To think. Right now, the police station was the safest place she could be. The problems would start when she left there. She just needed time to figure how to get out of town later without Niko following.

It wasn't until she was seated in the front seat of his unmarked car that the realization hit her, leaving a cold trail of fear in its wake.

Even if she managed to leave Niko behind, Jack would still be here. And if Rassi thought Jack had a clue to her whereabouts, Jack was as good as dead.

Nausea churned in her stomach, and she leaned forward, hauled in some air. Niko would go after Jack only if he discovered they had a relationship, she assured herself. There was no way for him to find that out, was there? But there was still Jolie. And Dace. If Niko stuck around long enough to learn what he could about Lindsay's life here, he was bound to learn of those relationships. And he'd be ruthless about using the knowledge to discover Lindsay's whereabouts.

Tears stung her eyes at the thought. Ties always brought complications. Hadn't she learned that over the years? They drew innocent parties into Niko's path. People who would still be alive if it weren't for their connection with her.

Jack opened the door, slid into the car. His voice was gruff. Grudging. "Are you okay?"

"There's no good end to this. Just drive me to the interstate. I'll get a lift. And all this will go away." She lifted her head, looked at him then. Saw her answer in his expression and nearly wept. "Stop thinking like a cop for one minute, that's all I ask. You can't fix this. You can't change it. And I'm sorrier than you could possibly imagine for getting you mixed up in it."

A stillness had come over Jack. His expression gave nothing away, but the intensity of his focus was unnerving. "Does 'it' have a name?"

Niko's name was on her lips, trembled there. And then in a flash of déjà vu, she was in New York City again, listening to her friends tell her what they'd discovered about Niko. What they'd shared with Detective Vickers. And forty-eight hours later she'd begun identifying her friends as they showed up in the morgue. One by one.

Fear froze her inclination to open up. Instead she swallowed hard and reached for enough to appease him. "I can't tell you that. Only that he buys and sells people, including police. He must have seen the newscast," she said bleakly, eyes staring blankly out the window. "He must have recognized me and tracked me down. I didn't get out soon enough. Now you and Dace and Jolie might be in danger because of me, and I…" Her voice hitched and she stopped, lips flattening as she summoned control. When she'd won the battle for it, she continued. "I promised myself I was never going to let that happen again."

There was a long silence but she could almost hear Jack mentally piecing together what she'd said. What she didn't say. Funny how she could predict his thought processes on the basis of their short acquaintance. And the realization that accompanied that knowing filled her with a sense of fatalism.

"Look at me." When she failed to do so, Jack reached out and tipped her face toward his with one finger beneath her chin. "I recognize the guy's a threat. And I don't doubt he's given you plenty of reason to fear him. But he isn't invincible. You have to trust me." When she tried to shake her head, he forestalled her protest. "You *have* to, Lindsay." Their gazes did battle for long moments. "Whoever this guy is, he nearly killed you today. Nearly killed both of us. How long have you been running? Six months? A year?"

Something on her face must have alerted him because he stopped, shock flickering in his expression. "Years, then." His hand dropped away from her face to curl in a ball in his lap. "A guy like that has a pretty powerful motivation. And I'm not underestimating the bastard. But you're underestimating *me* if you think for a second I'm going to let you run off to take your chances with him."

His movements as he started the car, put it in gear, were carefully controlled. Restraint layered over violence. And his implacable tone dashed any forlorn hope she held that he was going to help her make an escape. "There are other ways. There are programs—"

Lindsay gave a bitter laugh, her head leaning on the leather headrest. "You mean like Witness Protection? Where I take my chances that no one inside gets greedy and sells my information to the wrong person? I like my chances better on my own."

"You're short on trust. I get that. But sometimes it comes down to the devil you know. So you'd better think about doling out more of that story, Lindsay. Because if you think I'm letting you deal with this guy alone, Mitch's bullet did more damage to your head than I thought."

He'd lost control for a moment, and the situation had gone to hell.

Niko kept his binoculars trained on the scene in front of Gracie's place. From his hiding place under the large pine, he had an excellent vantage point from which to keep track of the cops' movements. And her location.

It was her fault, of course. Seeing her again, in the flesh, not just those seconds frozen by the camera, had rocked him more than he'd believed possible. Little, innocent Grace Feller. Even knowing what a lying, traitorous bitch she was hadn't stopped that surge of pure lust when he'd seen her again.

He wasn't finished with her. That's all it was. And seeing that guy go inside with her, stay long enough to leave no doubt as to what they were doing in there, okay, maybe that had messed up his thinking.

He'd almost capped the guy when he'd come out. Actually had started to squeeze the trigger, imagining his brains spattered all over the side of that garage. But he'd held back, hadn't he? Held off knowing that once the guy was gone, he'd have Gracie to himself. And then they'd have a long conversation about her leaving New York without his permission, taking something that belonged to him.

Rage was fogging his vision and he lowered the binoculars for a moment. He needed her alive long enough to tell him where she'd put it. Long enough for him to show her why it didn't pay to run out on Niko Rassi.

Yeah, and maybe just long enough for him to get another taste of her. All that white skin and those mile-long legs. Just a taste to prove to himself that she was out of his system before he killed her.

But the guy—the cop—hadn't left. And seeing them together, the way she let the pig put his hands on her...it would have served the whore right to take a bullet in the brain then and there. She was his. Would be until he said otherwise.

And when he did, his Magnum would do the talking.

The fury was still ripe enough to choke him, but he

shoved it down. Let it work for him. He'd missed a shell, but it couldn't be helped. He'd had to get out of there fast when that cop had come for him. And it pleased him that Gracie had seen it—and would know what it meant.

Raising the binoculars again, he trained them on the couple in the unmarked car. What was she telling him? Was she spilling her guts about New York? About him?

No, he decided after a moment. She was too scared for that. The bitch had never been stupid. She'd do what she'd done back then—lie and flutter those cat-green eyes of hers and then run first chance she got.

But he wasn't going to waste time chasing her up and down the coast. He had a business to run. And it didn't pay to be absent too long. Paulo Portino was a suspicious and impatient man.

So this ended, here, in this godforsaken city. Niko started to wiggle free of his hiding place beneath the low-hanging fir branches. He had to think through the details, but he knew exactly what would keep Gracie from running again.

He smiled, thinking of how it would play out. He'd get everything he wanted from her, and when he was finished there'd be once last shell with her name on it.

And this one wouldn't be wasted.

"Because she's lying, Captain." Jack paced Telsom's office, his frustration evident in his long strides. "She's running from someone and now he's found her. Those bullets were meant for her and all the denials in the world aren't going to convince me otherwise."

Jack might have been pissed, but he stopped short of telling Telsom everything: that Lindsay Bradford's ID was as shallow as the reflecting pond in Monument Park. He couldn't even say what was stopping him. He wanted to dig deeper into her secrets himself before he bared them to the world.

"Doesn't matter what she told you one-on-one," Telsom said implacably. "If her statement says she has no idea who might have shot at her, we are done with her. Kick her loose." He frowned, and Jack's instincts went on full red alert. "Unless… You aren't involved with her, are you?"

Damn, that question was becoming too familiar. And since it depended on how the captain defined *involved,* Jack gave him his best blank stare. "I told you, I happened by the hospital, her friend asked me to give her a ride home. End of story."

Telsom rubbed at the back of his neck. "People lie to us all the time. That's nothing new."

"Because she's scared." And he made damn sure that none of the emotion he was feeling sounded in his words. "Scared enough to run, and she's still a material witness in the Engels incident."

"Engels is dead, so it isn't as though we need her testimony." But Telsom was listening now. His black swivel chair creaked as he leaned back in it. "I can't give you any manpower on this, but if you want to keep an eye on her, that's on you. Give us time for ballistics to come back on the bullets recovered from today's scene, and maybe we'll get a little more information to confront her with. Just watch your step, Langley. The last thing we need is for her to start screaming police harassment, especially with the press ready to hang a medal on her for the restaurant incident."

Jack gave a curt nod and headed out the door. It wouldn't do for the captain to start inquiring any more closely about his relationship with Lindsay. Or maybe he should start thinking of her as *Gracie.*

He headed back to the interview room, his mood grim. Okay, so he'd known she had mysteries tucked away. That had been clear almost from the start. So maybe it shouldn't feel like such a punch in the gut that she refused to share them—all of them—after her past had made a head-on collision with her present this afternoon.

Chapter 8

Grace Feller, aka Sara Schmidt, aka Lori Altman, aka Cassie Richards, aka Lindsay Bradford, sat in the front seat of Jack's car with one hand braced on the dashboard and the other clutching the door handle. She still swayed from side to side every time Jack made an unsignaled turn.

Twisting in her seat as much as the seat belt would allow, she peered behind them. If Niko had managed to follow them from the police station, Jack's defensive driving would throw him off their trail.

Facing forward again, she noted Jack checking the rearview mirror. "Do we have a tail?"

"Not that I can see. But if he is back there, I'll make sure we lose him before heading home."

Home. The word sent a funny pang through her stomach. She'd readied herself for an argument when he'd rejoined her in the interview room. It had been pretty evident when he'd left that he'd been on the verge of strangling her. But he'd regained control before re-entering the room, surprising her with his matter-of-fact logic: if the shooter had followed them there, how did she expect to lose him on her own?

That question had been gnawing a hole inside her for the last hour. And because his suggestion made more sense than any idea she'd come up with, she'd reluctantly agreed to accompany him to his house, trusting Jack to shake any possible tail along the way.

Leaving town could be accomplished just as easily from Jack's place as from the police station. Waiting until he was asleep to sneak away would be low—her stomach roiled at the thought—but holing up at his place for long and chancing Niko tracking her there was far worse. She couldn't take the risk of Jack becoming collateral damage. Her conscience wouldn't withstand the burden of yet another life weighing on it.

A thought occurred then, had panic flaring. "How do you know he didn't plant a GPS locator on your car? He wouldn't have to follow closely then. He could hang back and track the car from a distance."

Jack slanted her a look. "Because he'd have to be pretty damn gutsy to plant a device on the car in the police station lot." He flipped on the revolving dash light and slowed at the next intersection, checking for traffic before running the red light.

It was several minutes before he spoke again. When he did, his tone was careful. "Fear can have a funny effect on our memories. It isn't unusual for victims to magnify their abuser's power over time, for instance. Whoever this guy is, Lindsay, whatever he's done, he's still just a man. He doesn't have superhuman capabilities."

She fought to suppress the wild laugh that rose to her throat. "You have no idea what he's capable of."

"Then tell me." All the frustration she'd sensed from him in the last few hours was pent up in the words. "I can't help if you won't tell me the whole story."

Her vision blurred. Stress and worry, she told herself, and willed her eyes to clear again. They'd covered and re-covered this ground a hundred different ways and they'd never agree.

"You're partially right," she murmured, her voice aching. "You can't help me."

An hour later, Lindsay wandered around Jack's town house, more curious than she would have liked to admit. She'd expected the glass and chrome, sleek lines and leather furniture. And certainly the big-screen TV was no shock, as men of all ages these days seemed to think they couldn't watch sports if the players didn't appear life-size on their screens.

But she hadn't expected the small, decorated Christmas tree that was tucked into one corner of the living room, several gaily wrapped packages beneath it. And the well-equipped kitchen was a surprise, with its black appliances and huge center countertop. A counter that looked well used, from the looks of the cutlery sitting on its surface and the pans hanging above it. The row of herbs growing on his windowsill had her shooting him an amazed look.

He lifted a shoulder. "I like to eat. Learning to cook was sort of self-defense." He hefted her bag, which he'd carried in from the car, and walked upstairs with it. Her nerves jittered at the sight, but she firmly calmed them. One step at a time. They'd given Niko the slip. Even she didn't believe anyone could have managed to follow them through the feints and turns and double-backs Jack had managed. Once he'd garaged his car, he'd humored her and thoroughly searched it and found no GPS device. So she'd take this opportunity to catch her breath.

And try to quell the inner voice telling her that Jack Langley might not be as easy to slip away from.

Pushing the thought away, Lindsay went to the large bowl of fruit on the center counter and selected an apple. The oddity of finding fresh fruit in a man's kitchen was second only to the feeling of displacement from being here at all. Hitching her hip on one of the stools lining one edge of the counter, she took a bite. She'd need nourishment to think, to plan her escape. Heck, who was she kidding? She'd need boatloads of luck, as well, something that had been in short supply for the last few years.

"I put your bag in the spare bedroom."

She started at Jack's voice behind her. For a big man he moved silently.

"You're eating. Good." He went to the refrigerator, opened the freezer compartment and scanned the contents. "You're going to need more than an apple to get your strength back. You haven't eaten since breakfast at the hospital this morning, have you?"

His words brought a sense of amazement. Was it only that morning she'd left the hospital? "No. But this is enough."

"For a four-year-old, maybe." He withdrew a package and put it in the microwave to thaw. Then he got out two large potatoes and started scrubbing them in the sink. "I owe you a dinner, anyway. How do you feel about steak?"

She opened her mouth to deny hunger but her stomach made a liar out of her. "Mildly interested, as it happens. What can I do to help?"

"Grab a bottle out of the wine rack, round up a corkscrew and pour us a couple glasses." As he spoke Jack wrapped potatoes in cellophane and turned on the oven. When the microwave dinged, he exchanged the potatoes for the meat and brought the package to the counter to unwrap it.

Lindsay studied him carefully. If she didn't know him better, she would believe he'd forgotten all about their bitter ongoing argument. That he'd put the events of the day behind him, in lieu of the juicy steaks he was busy unwrapping.

Unfortunately, she *did* know him better.

Slipping from the stool, she looked for the wine rack he'd indicated next to the refrigerator. Studying the labels, she selected a red she'd never heard of and started going through the drawers until she came up with a corkscrew.

Maybe nerves and rampant paranoia were to blame, but she had a hard time believing that Jack had moved on from their earlier disagreement. Fiercely she wrestled the cork from the bottle. He thought he'd soften her up, she decided. Feed her, get her tipsy, and then, when she was least expecting it, start pumping her for information again.

Just the thought had a wave of weariness hitting her. She extracted two wineglasses from a shelf above the wine rack and she carefully filled them. He'd discover her opinion unchanged, if that was the case. She opened her mouth to tell him that, but then closed it again.

There was just something so…*normal* about watching him move capably around the kitchen. Not that she'd ever experienced having a man cook for her, but she could almost imagine they were any other couple just getting to know each other.

Sliding his glass over to him, she ignored the stab of regret that came with the image. Nothing had been normal for her since leaving Wisconsin. Which was ironic, since she'd left in the first place because normal had equated with boring. Life there had been a stranglehold, every passing moment tightening its grip on her.

She sipped the wine, letting the memory wash over her in a shower of nostalgia. When she'd left Ellison, Wisconsin, she'd felt like she could breathe freely for the first time in her life. New York had embraced her, with its diversity and endless possibilities. She hadn't had to worry about not fitting in where everyone else seemed unique. There were no preconceived notions. No set boundaries so confining they threatened to choke her.

And once she'd crossed Niko Rassi, there had been no going home again.

The familiar pain swept over her, as sharp and ruthless as a blade. And because it didn't pay to think of all she'd lost, she shoved the memories aside, locked them away. She needed to concentrate on the now. And that meant making sure she didn't put anyone else at risk.

Cocking her head, she watched Jack season the meat from a shaker. "What's that?"

"My own special concoction. If I told you, I'd have to kill you. And since that seems a bit redundant under the circumstances, I'll keep the recipe to myself." Expertly he flipped the steaks onto the grill portion of the stove and turned it on.

Lindsay drank again, watching him carefully over the top of her wineglass, trying to gauge his mood. It wasn't anger in his tone. Not exactly. But there was something simmering inside him. Maybe not temper. But a steel core of determination.

With an inner sigh, she set the glass down, her fingers toying with the stem. The edge of exhaustion was crowding in, but resolutely she fought it back. She'd catch a few hours' sleep before she headed out tonight. She'd have to. Right now she felt like she'd do a face-plant if she so much as stood up too quickly.

Picking up the apple, she took another bite and used a tried-and-true trick she'd developed. Pushed away the fear, the weariness, the worry and concentrated on the moment. It was no hardship. Whatever his mood right now, Jack was a pleasure to watch, his hands sure, his movements lithe and fluid as he moved around the kitchen checking on the food. It would be so easy to just unload on him. To tell him everything and believe that he could fix it. That there was a way out that didn't include more death.

The wistful little fantasy spun out, gilding the moment. She let herself imagine that everything she'd put in motion three years ago was over. And she and Jack were free to discover if there was more between them than overactive hormones and combustible chemistry. No sense of urgency. No impending doom. The surge of longing that accompanied the mental image nearly stole her breath.

The shrill of a cell phone brought her back to reality with a jolt. She looked around, but Jack had carried her purse and bag upstairs.

He took his cell out of his pocket and checked the ID before sliding it across the counter toward her. "It's Jolie. I talked to Dace earlier about what happened this afternoon. I'm sure she'll want to speak to you."

Her gaze flew to his guiltily. Of course Jolie would have heard. And was probably going out of her head worrying. She picked up Jack's phone and flipped it open. "Jolie. I was going to call you later."

There was silence for a moment and then, "Lindsay? You're with Jack? Well, thank God for that. I've been calling your phone for the last half hour. Are you all right? Dace said neither of you were hit, but—"

"We're fine. I'm just not close to my phone." Supremely aware of the man nearby unabashedly listening to her side of the conversation, she turned half away from him. "Jack brought me to his place to feed me after I gave my statement."

"Good." The relief in her friend's voice fanned the guilt a little hotter. "I hope you aren't planning to go back to your apartment tonight."

"I'm been offered a room at Motel Langley for the night. I plan to take him up on it."

"We were worried about that. You really have no idea who might have been shooting at you?"

It was hard, very hard, to lie to her closest friend. "No. I guess the police will be looking into it, though."

"Dace and I are going to be tied up at the hospital for a while. I was going to offer our place, but if you're going to be with Jack, that's even better."

Something in the other woman's voice alerted her. "How is Trixie?"

"Always thought she was too mean to die." Jolie's voice shook a bit on the last word and she paused, as if collecting herself. When she continued again, her tone was steady. "But they're talking hospice after the next thirty-six hours, so there are lots of arrangements to be made."

"I'm sorry. I know it's been...complicated." She might not know all the details of Jolie's relationship with her mother, but she'd gleaned that much. "I wish I could do something."

"You can answer your phone next time you get shot at."

That drew a laugh. "I could, yes."

"I heard about the engraved shell. It could just be a case

of mistaken identity, but until we're sure it'd be best for you to stick close to Jack."

"Well, I'm in his kitchen watching him make me dinner." She spun around on the stool to look at him. "Can't get much closer than that." Now was no time to recall—was it only hours ago?—when they'd been as close as two people could get. A flush of heat crawled up her neck. It almost seemed as if those moments had existed outside of time. But it hadn't taken long before reality had intruded.

"Stay put until they figure out what's going on. Here's the doctor. I have to go. Talk to you tomorrow."

"Bye." There was an oddly hollow feeling in the pit of her stomach as Lindsay disconnected the call. Realizing she wouldn't see her friend again added another fang to the regret gnawing through her.

And knowing it was better this way—safer for everyone—didn't lessen the pain appreciably.

"Trouble?" Jack got out two plates and removed the baked potatoes from the microwave, setting one on each dish.

She handed his phone back to him. "Sounds like Jolie's mother isn't going to last much longer."

"Yeah, Dace said. Good riddance."

Shocked, her gaze flew to his. Looking up from the steaks he was serving up, he shrugged. "Jolie's told you about Trixie, right?"

"A little." He went to put a steak on her plate and she protested quickly, "No. Not the whole thing. I can't eat all that...." She reached out for her plate but it was too late. A rib eye fit for a football player was placed next to the potato and the plate nudged over to her.

Jack handed her silverware. "You need your strength. Eat."

Dubiously, she eyed the food even as she cut off a piece of steak. If she ate like this every day she'd need a forklift to get up the stairs to her apartment. Not that she was planning to return there, anyway.

She took a bite of the meat. Chewed. Then closed her eyes in ecstasy. The meat was tender. Succulent. Lindsay concentrated on the individual flavors, trying to identify what he'd added to the seasoning. Swallowing, she cut another bite. "This is excellent. What'd you say was in that seasoning?"

He dumped enough margarine on his potato to have his arteries slamming shut in protest. "I didn't say. But if you're interested in an information exchange, we could probably work something out."

When she went silent, he gave a sardonic smile. "No? Why am I not surprised?"

Ignoring his sarcasm, she concentrated on the meal. "What did you mean about Jolie's mother? She's never said much to me, but I could tell their relationship is rocky."

"Rocky." He picked up his glass for a drink of wine before continuing. "You could say that. I don't know the whole thing. Bits and pieces from what Dace says. But apparently Trixie was an addict. Jolie landed in foster care when she was just a kid. Bounced around a lot. By the time her mother contracted cancer she was living on the streets. Jolie took her in a few months ago, but the old lady's been a handful. Selling everything she can steal from their apartment for a fix. It's been an ordeal, for everyone involved."

A wave of sympathy for her friend hit Lindsay. Whatever the complications of her relationship with her mother, Jolie had traumatic times ahead of her. Times when she could use the support of a friend. But Lindsay would be gone.

There was a twist to her stomach at the thought. Better to be gone, she told herself stoutly, than to bring Niko Rassi into everyone's life, especially at a time when Jolie would be distracted. Vulnerable. Better for everyone if Lindsay headed far, far away, hopefully drawing Niko after her. The thought had goose bumps prickling her skin.

Jack got up and went into the other room, returning a moment later with a throw from the couch. He draped it around her shoulders. "Better?"

She could only nod. The simple act of kindness had her eyes burning. He'd done far more for her than she had any right to expect. And yes, she had no doubt he was merely biding his time before attempting to pry more information from her, but that was the cop in him. He couldn't help himself. It still touched her, more than it should have, to discover layers in the man. Sexy. Tough. Bullheaded. Generous. And now, tender.

She didn't want to reveal the emotions swimming too close to the surface, so she concentrated on finishing her meal. Or as much of it as she could. Shutting down thought and emotion to concentrate on the simple act of eating. Jack was right. She was going to need her strength.

She was also going to need an incredible streak of luck.

His cell rang again as she was getting up to clear the dishes. She loaded the dishwasher and wiped the counters. Other than a cryptic "Interesting" and "Anything else?" he was mostly listening, as he cleaned the grill-top implement he'd used to cook the steaks. He didn't so much as glance in her direction, and some of the tension began to ease from her muscles. Maybe now would be the time to excuse herself and slip upstairs. Scout the exits and plan her escape for later that night.

She sent him a sideways glance. It was nearly eight. Early, but with the day she'd had it wouldn't seem unusual to plead weariness and head to her room for the evening. Nor would it be that far from the truth. She'd set her phone to silent alarm so its vibration would wake her at two. And while Jack was sleeping she'd be on the run again.

Just the thought had exhaustion edging to the surface. But she beat it back, waited for Jack to get off the phone before saying, "I'm not sure how much longer I can remain standing." That, at least, was the truth. "If you'll show me where I'm sleeping tonight, I think I'll turn in."

His dark gaze was enigmatic as it fixed on hers for a long moment. But his tone, when he spoke, was even. "Sure. Follow me." They went down a short hall and then up the stairs, past one door. He indicated the next one. "You can use this bathroom. Your room is across the hall."

She glanced around before turning to her door. Only one window in the hallway. The placement of the bathroom meant there'd be none in it. She opened the door to the second bedroom and was relieved to see two windows.

She let the blanket slip from her shoulders and folded it. Handing it to him, she began, "I want to thank you…"

He waved off her words. "It's not necessary. I'll let you get ready to turn in and check on you later."

Her earlier relief was dampened a smidgen. "No, you don't need to do that. Like I said, I'm just going to fall into bed."

"It's no problem."

She watched him withdraw from the doorway and saunter down the hall, felt a tug of unease. Damn. Now she'd have to take the time to change into something resembling sleepwear, rather than catching a few hours in the clothes she meant to escape in. It meant she'd lose valuable minutes when she woke because she'd have to change again before leaving.

She went to the bathroom and brushed her teeth. Washed her face. Wondering the whole time at Jack's easy capitulation. She'd expected him to wait until she was off guard before starting to push and pry again. It would be a mistake to lower her defenses.

Padding back across the hall to the bedroom, she noted that it would be an even bigger error to think about their proximity. About the fact that after a few hours she was never going to see him again. And it was a huge mistake to let the sorrow from the thought well up in her until the tide of emotion threatened to drown her good sense. Her better judgment.

Swiftly, she changed into a tee and yoga pants. They looked enough like sleepwear, she judged, but she could still wear them when she left later and save herself a few minutes. She didn't know whether or not Jack was a light sleeper. If he was, the less she moved around in here prior to leaving, the better.

When the knock sounded at her door, she opened it to find Jack lounging against the doorjamb. "Find everything you need?"

Nerves jittered in her stomach. He'd used the intervening time to strip down to his jeans, as if he were planning on an early night, too.

Or as if he were planning on joining her in the guest bed.

Firmly, she shoved that errant thought aside. "Everything's fine. I was just going to turn in."

"Did you take your medication?"

She hadn't.

"I'll get you a glass of water."

Blowing out a breath, she picked up her purse and

started rifling through it. She'd shoved the bag of supplies in the bottom of it, she recalled, along with her money and her... She dug deeper into the purse, and then dumped it on the bed beside her, disbelief warring with panic.

"I took the liberty of removing a few items when I brought your things upstairs." Jack crossed the room and set the glass of water on the bedside table, then leaned against the dresser, watching her knowingly.

Panic morphed to temper in one smooth stroke. Lindsay's jaw clenched. She'd known he wasn't one to give in easily. And she'd learned only a few hours ago that he was cursed with a suspicious nature. "Where's my gun? And my money?"

"They're safe. But I thought you might think twice about sneaking out of here if I held on to both of them for you."

"You had no right!" She pushed away from the bed and in two long strides was inches away from him. "Get them for me now. Or I'll take this place apart looking for them."

"How about an exchange?" The lopsided smile he gave her was marred by his steely tone. "I'll tell you where they are. You tell me why Niko Rassi is after you."

Chapter 9

The floor seemed to buckle beneath Lindsay's feet. Roaring filled her ears. A knot formed in her throat and grew until it threatened to choke her. "I..." She could barely manage speech around it. "I don't know what you mean."

"Bull." Jack clapped a hand on her shoulder and walked her backward until the backs of her knees met the bed. She didn't resist when he forced her to sit. Her knees didn't feel all that reliable. Where could he have gotten Niko's name? How?

"He does the wet work for the Portino family, right? Connected New York mob outfit. Runs some sort of nightclub there, but his real source of income comes from the hits." His staccato delivery hammered at her guard, as she struggled for comprehension. "How did you ever run afoul of the Portino family? Did you work for them?"

Lindsay moistened her lips. "No."

He stared hard at her, the intensity of those dark eyes searing her. "Well, you crossed them some way, or they regard you as a threat. That's the only reason I can think of for them to send their contracted killer after you."

The rapid-fire questions calmed something inside her. He knew a bit but he didn't know all. There was a way around this. She just needed time to think. "I don't know what you're talking about. Where are you getting all this?"

He curled his lip. "Save it. That phone call earlier? It was a buddy at the precinct. I had him run the MO of using an engraved shell through a few databases and he came up with some interesting stuff. Seems there's a raft of unsolved homicides in the New York City area, going back as far as nine years. He put a call in to a detective working one of the cases who said they've been pulling bodies out of the rivers there for nearly a decade. Guess what they have in common? A bullet hole in the forehead and a shell with the vic's name engraved on the side, tucked somewhere in their clothing."

An eerie sense of calm came over her then. She deliberately widened her eyes, looked at him bewilderedly. "Then whoever shot at me today must have me mistaken for someone else. I've never even been to New York."

He stared hard at her for a moment. "You're good," he said grudgingly. "Bet you've had some practice at it. But I'm better. The bullets they took out of the New York vics all match. They were all hand-loaded, which means the shooter is a bit of a fanatic about his work. Once ballistics gets done with the bullets dug out of the railing outside your place, how long do you think it will be before we match them to the ones taken from the other victims?"

Lindsay put a hand to her head, only half feigning weakness. The pounding there had nothing to do with her head wound, however, and everything to do with the information he was hammering her with. "I...don't understand. None of this makes any sense. My head... I need to lie down."

"Later." Taking her chin between his fingers, he turned her chin to face him and surveyed her grimly. "It's time to give it to me straight. The whole story, not just the bits and pieces you fed me this afternoon. It's the only way for me to help you, don't you get that? I can't protect you if I don't know what the hell is going on."

There was a light in his eye, a dangerous burn. "Let's start with your real name. Which is it? Grace Amundson? Grace Feller? Grace Remson? Grace Strickland? Grace Trumbell?" She stared at him numbly as he ticked off the list of names. It was like watching a house of cards fall in slow motion. Remove just one from the middle and the entire structure collapses in on itself.

"How..." Her voice was barely audible, so she swallowed, tried again. "Where did you get those names?"

He looked satisfied and she knew she'd answered at least one of his questions. "The National Center for Missing Adults has five listings for women of your approximate age with the first name of Grace. Most of them also have a picture. Do I need to call Phillips back, have them fax the photos to me?"

Feeling suddenly ancient, her hand went to his where it still held her chin, and pushed it away. If she had the strength she'd get up. Move away from him. But she doubted her legs would hold her. Her family had reported her missing. How odd that with all the subterfuge she'd engaged in to keep them safe, that single act had never occurred to her. "Grace Feller," she whispered.

Just the sound of the name whistled through her mind,

a snippet from the past. It sounded foreign, even to her ears. She'd ceased being Grace Feller over three years ago. And she'd begun cutting the ties three years before that.

"Feller." He thought a moment. "From Wisconsin, right?"

"This isn't solving anything." Somehow she summoned the strength to push away from the bed and carefully stepped around him to pace. She recognized the spurts of adrenaline firing through her veins. Knew that they could fade as suddenly as they'd appeared, and her system would finally crash. She needed to get some sleep. But she also knew there was no more avoiding Jack.

Which meant she'd have to tell him all, or most, and convince him he couldn't help her. That no one could.

Nerves clashed inside her like grinding gears in a car. "I told you this afternoon he was dangerous."

He blew out a breath. "Yeah, but somehow I didn't figure connected. How long have you been running from him?"

"Thirty-eight months," she said bleakly. And two weeks. Five days. She hooked a finger in the edge of the blind covering the window, lifted it to look out. Dark clouds scudded across the night sky, but her attention was on the ground below. Too far to jump. But there was an attached garage that the other window should look out over. She could safely land on that, then shimmy down a drain spout.

"So the Portino family put a contract out on you nearly three years ago, and you've been evading Rassi ever since." She heard the incredulity in Jack's voice. "Lady, with luck like that, you should be in Vegas."

Dropping the blind, she turned to face him. He was half twisted around to look at her, one knee on the bed. "Looks like my luck ran out about the time the restaurant incident made national news. And the Portino family doesn't have anything to do with this." At least she couldn't imagine how they would be involved. "It's just Niko." And that was more than enough.

She saw the questions in his expression, quickly followed by understanding. Recognized the impassive mask that shifted over his face and felt her heart sink a little further.

"It's personal, then."

"You could say that." She heard her voice come, as if from a distance. "Everything you said about him…it's all suspicion. The police have never been able to tie Niko to any of the murders. But I stole something from him that links him to six of them, and he wants it back. And he wants me dead for betraying him."

In the sudden silence she could hear the rain start, each individual raindrop plopping against the window. It'd be a wet walk to the interstate if it didn't stop. Somehow she couldn't summon the energy to care.

"What do you have, Lindsay?"

"The memory card from his digital camera." She'd stashed it in a safe spot before fleeing New York City. But she had no real illusions that Niko couldn't get that information out of her before killing her. She knew what he was capable of.

She crossed her arms, rubbing her suddenly chilled skin. "He likes to keep mementos of his kills. Ego, I guess. He's got plenty of that. He lays the engraved shell on the victim's chest, goes down on one knee next to the head, and takes the picture." Revulsion filled her, as hot and strong as the first time Ricky had showed her the photos he'd recovered on the camera she'd let him borrow. "Stupid on his part."

Jack nodded. "But not that unusual. Lots of serial offenders take souvenirs. They use them to relive the thrill of the kill afterward. You say you recovered the pictures?"

She didn't answer him directly. It seemed important that he understand. After she was gone, she wanted him to at least know the why.

"There were four of us. Wendy—she and I graduated at semester of our senior year and cut out for New York." No amount of ultimatums or pleas from either of their parents had had any effect. They'd planned their escape from Ellison since they were fifteen. "We met Ricky our first year in the city, Nathan our second. We hung together. Looked out for each other. Couldn't afford places to live on our own, so we shared a studio apartment." She gave a short laugh at the memory. "It was halfway to New Jersey and the size of a shoebox, but it was ours."

"And then you met Niko."

He was good at this, she realized. At listening and drawing out and letting the story spin at its own pace. He had practice with his job. And she hated, violently, the idea that she had become just that to him. Part of the job.

"Not then. Not until I'd been in the city for a couple years. Nathan was older and we were going out to clubs to celebrate his twenty-first birthday." How young they were then. There was an odd sort of pain at the memory. Lindsay leaned a shoulder against the closet door. Young and exuberant and invincible. Life was a journey and every day was a new adventure.

"We'd finessed our way into Kouples, although Nathan was the only one old enough. The rest of us couldn't get served. The bartender called security on us when we tried. Just when we were being shown to the door, Niko intervened."

She knew now he'd watched the whole thing from his lair in his office. He'd told her often enough how he'd been mesmerized the moment he'd set eyes on her. For too long that had charmed her. Eventually it had terrified her.

She lifted a shoulder. "He dazzled us. Set us all up with drinks and invited us to join him in his private booth. He was…attracted."

"I'll bet." Jack's tone was clipped. "He must have been a decade older."

"He was sophisticated and engaging, with an aura of polished danger that I found irresistible." It was impossible to keep the self-condemnation from her voice. "He gave us all jobs and it wasn't long before he was the center of my world. I thought he was a club owner. By the time we found out different it was too late. For all of us."

"Okay. These others you mentioned…your friends? They can verify your story?"

She should have been prepared for the question. Instead the pain ambushed her again, a keen-edged agony that time had failed to dull. Unable to speak, Lindsay just shook her head. She had to force the words from her lips. "They're all dead. Niko killed them."

Lindsay saw Jack spring across the room. Had a moment to note once again how fast the man could move. His arms were closing around her before she even realized her knees had given out. He scooped her up before she crumpled to the floor, turned and strode to the bed, setting her down to lean against the headboard and then propping the pillows behind her.

"You've had enough hits today to send most people reeling," he muttered. "You need sleep. The rest of this can wait until tomorrow."

It couldn't, of course. Because she wouldn't be here

tomorrow. With or without the money and the gun, she'd be long gone before Jack ever awakened. But now he'd understand why. And that brought her a modicum of peace.

"I'll finish it. There isn't much more."

Jack stood there indecisively, as if unsure whether he should insist. But then he sat down on the bed, moving her legs so they lay across his lap.

The intimacy of their position made her feel awkward. She wasn't used to being taken care of, although in her naiveté she'd mistaken Niko's possessiveness for something similar. She'd made all sorts of mistakes with Niko, worn blinders for far too long.

"Rick was the techie. Niko had him working with the video surveillance for the club, but he knew computers, too. Cameras. Cell phones. He'd gotten his hands on some photo-recovery software and he was hot to try it out. But none of us owned a camera. I knew where Niko kept his, though." She swallowed hard. "I thought, what's the harm, you know? It wasn't like Ricky was even going to take the camera out and use it. He was just going to learn how the software worked, recover the photos that had been deleted from the memory card, delete them again."

"But he recovered photos of the kills." Jack's thumb went to the arch of her foot and rubbed, and she had to stifle a moan. A woman didn't make her living on her feet and not appreciate the pleasure of a good foot rub.

"Ricky went to Nathan first. And then Wendy. It was days before they came to me. I didn't believe them at first. But Ricky had printed the pictures. I couldn't argue with that."

But she'd wanted to. They'd researched the identities of the people in the photos, and she still remembered how desperately she'd wanted to discover some other explanation. Even though she was already beginning to realize

Niko Rassi wasn't the man she'd thought he was, believing he was a killer was still impossible. Until the research had proved her wrong.

"Nathan and Ricky talked us into letting them go to the police alone. They spoke to a Detective Lee Vickers. He took the pictures and assured them that we'd be safe. But he needed time, he said. Twenty-four hours to put the case together. He said they had to go back to the club, pretend everything was normal. He'd contact them when he was ready to make the arrest."

Jack's fingers stilled on her foot. "He never contacted any of you?"

"I called him two days later and he denied ever seeing any pictures. Claimed the guys had only come in to report a robbery, and that he had the notes to prove it." The cold core of betrayal still burned. "He must have gone to Niko. Accepted a payoff. Maybe Niko's still paying him. All I know is, within thirty-six hours, Wendy, Nathan and Ricky couldn't be found. At first I thought Nathan had gotten scared and taken off. But then when Ricky didn't show up for work…and Wendy…" She'd been wild with worry. And all the while she'd been under Rassi's watchful eye. Trying to pretend everything was normal. Striving to act as though she didn't want to scream every time he touched her.

"And then they started pulling the bodies of my friends out of the East River." She closed her eyes tight, as if by doing so she could will the images out of her mind. Going to the morgue. IDing the bodies. And wondering if there was a photo somewhere of Niko kneeling next to each of their corpses.

She opened her eyes then, caught Jack's intense dark gaze on her and thought she read condemnation there. Or maybe it was just her own sense of guilt that projected it.

"I had nowhere to turn. I didn't dare go to the police. Not again. Niko waited until we'd returned from Nathan's funeral service before telling me he knew the whole thing."

She could still feel the crack of his fist across her face, knocking her to the floor. Could still recall looking up at him as he stood above her, straddling her with that cold hard smile on his face. And then he'd bent down to grab her by the hair and pulled her up to read the engraving on the shell he'd taken from his pocket.

This one has your name on it, Gracie. Tell me where it is, and maybe I won't use it.

"It's not your fault." Jack shook her leg a little as if to punctuate his statement. "They didn't die because of you, Lindsay. You can't take that on yourself."

She leaned her head back on the pillows and wished she could believe him. If it hadn't been for Niko's obsession with her, none of them would have had jobs at Kouples. None of them would have crossed Niko's path. So how could it not be her fault?

"He wanted the memory card but he couldn't be certain Nathan and Rick had told me about the pictures. So he took his time. Terrorized me for days." Woke her nightly from a dead sleep with curses and blows, she recalled. Or worse, far worse, when he'd pretended nothing was wrong and expected her to accept his advances, as if nothing had changed. "There was a part of him that wanted to believe me when I swore I didn't know anything about it. But I knew it was just a matter of time before he used that bullet on me."

"How'd you get away from him?" Jack's tone was tight, but that barely registered. She was lost in the grip of the past now, unable to shake free of its fetters.

"He had someone watching all the exits to the apartment

building when he wasn't there. The only way out was the roof." So she'd taken a gun, the memory card and what cash he'd had in his desk. And she'd gone upstairs and taken a chance on certain death, or a slim chance. "I managed to jump to the next rooftop, and went down a fire escape. He's never gotten close until now."

"And the memory card?"

"It's in a safe place."

It didn't escape Jack that she didn't answer his question. The hell of it was, he couldn't blame her. She'd been let down by the very system that should have protected her. He believed that, even though there was no way she'd be able to prove it. But he'd been around long enough to know corrupt cops existed, rotting the system from the inside out until they were extracted like the tumors they were.

His mind was racing. There had to be a way to finish this thing, to scoop up Rassi right here in Metro City. They had the bullets dug out of Lindsay's railing, and if they could match them to any gun they took off Rassi when they arrested him, they could at least pin him with attempted murder. If they got real lucky, they'd match the shell to the others in his possession as well as to the ones found on the New York victims, and tie him up in a neat bow that even the Portino family lawyer couldn't get him out of.

There was a helluva lot of planning before they were at that point, but the first issue to take care of was the woman lying next to him. The one who'd been preparing to run from the moment he'd brought her home a couple hours earlier. The one he was beginning to be able to read, and wasn't that a scary thing for someone he'd only met days ago?

She nudged him with her foot. "So I answered your question. You promised to give me my money and gun back."

Carefully, he lifted her feet out of his lap and stretched

out beside her, propping himself on one elbow. He observed the quick flicker across her expression and wondered at it. Fear? Desire? Or maybe that was wishful thinking because it was a little tougher than it should be to ignore their position. Their proximity. Their surroundings.

"They're in my gun closet."

"And now you'll return them."

"Actually—" time to tread lightly here "—I believe I said I'd tell you where they are. I did. Won't do you any good, though, because I have the key." Muscles tense, he prepared himself for temper. He wasn't disappointed.

She came off the pillows to slap both hands against his chest and give him an ungentle push. "I'm not going to be bullied by the likes of you, Langley. I've been taking care of myself for a long time now, and I don't need you trying to call the shots."

"Done a damn fine job of it, too," he said mildly. "If you don't count that psycho killer on your heels." Quick reflexes saved him from her first punch. But her sneaky left jab landed in his gut before he managed to capture both wrists in one of his hands. When she would have struggled he simply leaned over her, trapping her hands between their torsos.

"Think I don't know you plan on taking off the minute my back is turned?" The mutinous flash in her eyes told him he'd nailed her intentions dead on. "It's a race you can't win, don't you get that? With the money he's got, he has resources at his disposal you can't outrun. Someday you're going to turn around and he's going to be standing there with a gun aimed at your head. And that will be the end."

"And what are the alternatives? Wait around until

someone I care about gets killed instead? I've played those cards before, remember?" Her voice was tinged with bitterness. "As long as Niko's focused on me, he isn't hurting anyone else. I can live with that."

"It doesn't have to be one or the other." There had to be another way. He needed time to think, dammit, and being pressed up against Lindsay this way wasn't exactly conducive to productive brain functioning. He could feel her breasts brush his skin with each shallow rise and fall of her chest and the sensation hurtled him back to earlier that day when there'd been nothing between them. Just skin pressed against skin. Heat to heat.

He shifted uncomfortably. That was definitely not the direction his thoughts should be taking right now. "While we're waiting on ballistics we can contact the airports. Get their passenger manifests. If we can prove Rassi is here, once you tell your story to the captain he'll issue a BOLO, and the guy won't move without alerting someone on the force." He'd have to find a place to stash Lindsay in the meantime. With someone watching her so she didn't run and so Rassi couldn't get to her.

Of course, he mused, if the prick had used a false ID to hop a plane, they'd have to wait on ballistics to verify his presence in Metro City. Unless…

"Quickest way to convince the captain is to show him the photos on that memory card."

"That'll be tough, since it's in New York. Safe." When he sent her a narrowed look, she glared back at him. "By not carrying it with me, I still had a bargaining chip if Niko ever found me. To buy me time."

Smart, he thought grudgingly. He'd never denied she was smart. Although from what he'd heard, Rassi would take great pleasure in torturing the location of the card from her. A phone call to one of his flunkies back in New York and he'd have what he wanted. And Lindsay would be of no more use to him.

There was no point in running that scenario for her. So, he'd work the details out tonight. Maybe give Dace a call after Lindsay fell asleep from sheer exhaustion. Bounce a few ideas off him.

As if reading his thoughts, she said, "You have to promise that Jolie and Dace won't hear about this."

Something tightened inside him. "Ever think what this would have done to them if you'd left without a word? Jolie would have been out of her mind. As if she doesn't have enough on her plate right now."

The sheen that came to her eyes then, knowing he'd put it there, had remorse stabbing through him. Her body heaved beneath his, as she battled to free her hands. "Do you think I don't know that? That I haven't thought of it? I should have left days ago. I *knew* it was time to move on. And I also knew it was a mistake to have ties. Friends are a vulnerability I can't afford."

He subdued her easily, held her until she finally went limp. Her face turned away, but he could still see the struggle for control. Watched her fight that battle inch by inch and win. And it stirred a new emotion inside him that was as unusual as it was foreign. Respect.

Her voice, when it came, was low. Almost defeated. "Anyone I care about can be used against me. Niko proved that in New York. That's why I haven't contacted my family through all of this. That was the first place he'd look for me. But he can't use them to get to me if I'm not in touch. What would be the point of hurting them if I didn't know? I check the town newspaper on the Internet occasionally. They're all still safe. And they'll stay that way as long as I don't reach out. Just like Jolie and Dace will be once I'm gone." Her eyes met his then. "And you."

There was the slightest tremble to her full lower lip on those final words. And he wanted, desperately, to cover it with his own. Because the mental image of her drifting from one town to the next, always looking over her shoulder, never letting anyone too close, branded itself on his mind. Had something clutching inside his chest.

He needed to keep a clear head. The sliver of logic pierced the emotion clouding his judgment. There was a fraction of an inch between their mouths. He could feel every breath she released. And his muscles went tense with the inner struggle raging through him.

The last thing he needed right now was to fog the issue with sex. Because there wasn't a doubt in his mind where a kiss would lead. He'd already had a taste of Lindsay and he knew he wouldn't stop. Not until he had her stripped beneath him. Not until he was buried deep inside her again.

He clenched his jaw, damned his hormones. "You want to protect us. But you won't let anyone try and protect you."

The tip of her tongue moistened her lips and his body jerked in response. "You can't change my mind. I promised myself thirty-eight months ago that no one else was going to die because of me. That would be unforgivable."

He shifted, drew her hands above her head. And froze for a moment at the position of his body over hers. Too close to the way he imagined. Much too close.

He felt her body soften. Her eyelids lowered, her lips parting softly. He hauled in a breath, fought a fierce battle for willpower. "No more unforgivable than this."

Her eyes snapped open at the exact moment he closed the bracelet around her wrist. Locked it. He had the good sense to move swiftly out of the way before Lindsay bolted upright, pulling at the handcuff securing her to the headboard.

"Langley! You bastard!"

"Among other things." He rolled to the side of the bed and rose, carefully, his body a riot of clamoring urges. He didn't trust himself to look at her, so he rounded the bed, headed for the door. "I figure you'll be good and pissed by morning. But you'll still be alive. For now, I'll settle for that."

Chapter 10

Jack leaned a shoulder against the doorjamb of Lindsay's bedroom door and watched her sleep. There was a slight frown between her brows, as if even slumber hadn't muted her temper. He wouldn't doubt it. She'd been as angry as he'd ever seen her. Couldn't blame her there.

He sipped from the mug of coffee he'd brought for her. He'd already drunk two cups waiting for her to wake up. Of course, given the day she had yesterday, she ought to be comatose for hours yet. She ought to be a lot of things.

That she'd managed to evade a professional assassin for three years was nothing short of a miracle. But he didn't kid himself that it had come without a price. No friends. No contact with family. A new city and a new identity every few months. What the hell kind of life was that?

A lonely one. Jack's hand tightened on the mug. One full of fear and paranoia. And one destined to come to a very bad end if she kept on running. A woman living off the grid was vulnerable in a host of ways. Especially one who didn't trust the police. Rassi wasn't the only danger Lindsay'd had to worry about.

But not anymore. One way or another, she was through running.

It'd take some careful finessing. He scratched his jaw absently, was reminded he hadn't yet shaved. The favor he'd called in earlier this morning had already gotten the ball rolling. Jack didn't know anyone in ballistics, but Steve Riley, a buddy from the academy, did, and Riley owed him one. His friend had promised to get the analysis fast-tracked. If the markings on the shell casing and the bullets matched those in the database for the New York victims, at the very least it gave them a link to a contract killer.

Didn't give them Rassi, since the NYPD had only supposition about his activities. His name on an airline manifest would help, but that couldn't be counted on.

The photos would be the kicker. But until they could get to them he was betting Captain Telsom would be interested enough in Lindsay's story to arrange protection. He just had to figure out how to make her stay put long enough to accept it. Although the idea of keeping her handcuffed to one of his beds was not without charm, it wasn't feasible for the long term.

Be hard to explain to Telsom, for one thing. Especially since he'd assured him there was nothing personal between him and Lindsay.

He crossed one bare foot over the other and watched her sleeping form broodingly. It wasn't a lie. Not technically. Yeah, okay, so he was a little wrapped up in keeping her alive. He was a cop. That's what he did. And maybe they'd only known each other four days, but it'd been a helluva four days. With all the baggage she was carrying, he was bound to feel…protective. He took another sip of her coffee, satisfied with the word. Yeah, that was it exactly. There wasn't a woman alive who could get to him this fast. But life and death had a way of intensifying a situation until it was hard to separate the drama from stickier emotions. He just had to keep that in mind.

Lindsay stirred once. Then her eyes opened, instantly focused, alert and fixed on him. And the punch-in-the-gut sensation he got made a mockery of his earlier thoughts.

He held up the mug like the peace offering it was. "I brought you coffee."

"Do you feel like wearing it?"

Since he didn't especially, he stayed where he was. "Still mad, huh?"

"Unless you're wearing a cup, I wouldn't advise coming over to see." The glare she shot him would take the strongest man out at the knees. "The only thing I want from you is the key to these." She held up her wrist as much as she was able.

Since she didn't seem interested in the coffee, he took another drink. "We need to come to an agreement."

"You mean like where I don't report you for kidnapping and false imprisonment in return for my gun and money?"

"I mean where you agree to accept police protection." He forestalled what was certain to be a hot response by adding, "Because if the only way to keep you safe is to lock you up until you come to your senses, that can be arranged."

She scooted up in bed and shoved her free hand through her mussed hair. His eyes tracked the movement. He'd taken her to bed, but he'd never slept with her. Never wakened with her. She looked good, all rumpled, mussed and riled. It was all too easy to imagine being in that bed with her. Being the one to smooth that heavy fall of hair back from her face and kiss the sulk from her lips.

With effort, he brought his mind back to the matter at hand. "The way I see it, I've got a problem."

"And yet *I'm* the one wearing handcuffs. Go figure."

"I've got to go to work. And since I can't trust you to be here when I get back, we've got two choices. You can agree to come in and tell Captain Telsom what you told me last night." He thought it best to ignore the rude sound she made at that. "Or I can haul you in and lock you up."

Lindsay gaped at him. "For what? Accepting 'hospitality' from a lunatic?"

"Carrying a concealed weapon without a permit. False identification." He noted the flicker of expression on her face and pressed, "Unless you're ready to tell the captain what you told me, you can't be identified. For all we know you could be a felon. Might have a record. Could take a while to sort it all out."

He fancied he could hear her grinding her teeth. "You already figured out who I was, remember?"

Cocking his head, he said, "Did I? Don't seem to recall that. Bet it would take a day or two to rediscover it."

"Why are you doing this?"

"I'm trying to keep you alive. You could stay here, where Rassi can't find you. Or you can stay behind bars, where he can't get at you. Either way works. Your choice."

The suggestion she made then was imaginative, if unladylike. He grinned. "Don't make me get the soap." He heard the distinctive ring of his cell downstairs. "Take a few minutes to think it over."

"Don't you walk out here. Jack! Unlock these handcuffs first!"

Jogging down the stairs, he considered that he'd better step outside to take the call. If the caller overheard what Lindsay was shouting after him, it could be difficult to explain.

But the short phone conversation that ensued managed to douse his earlier humor. Sober, he retraced his steps and returned to the spare bedroom. One look at his expression and whatever snotty remark she'd been about to make slid down her throat.

"What is it?"

"That was Darrell, our PPA. He just fielded a phone call from a woman claiming to be your mother."

The emotions flashing over her expression were easily identified. Shock. Disbelief. Joy. And most puzzling, wariness. "What did she say?"

"That you'd been missing for years and she'd recently learned the Metro City PD knew of your whereabouts. Darrell said he'd take a message and get it to the appropriate detective. He must have found out that was me."

"She didn't say anything else?"

"Not that he mentioned."

She took a deep breath, released it slowly. "Call him back."

Her reaction was puzzling. "You don't want to talk to your mom first?"

"Not until I find out how she discovered I'm in California."

To humor her, he pulled out his cell and pressed Redial. "Lindsay, your face was on CNN, remember? Unless you're going to tell me they don't have TVs in Wisconsin, it's pretty easy to figure out how she knew where to find you."

"Unless things have changed in the last half dozen years, TV isn't allowed in our house."

"Darrell." Jack crossed to the bed, sat down beside Lindsay. "The call you took earlier regarding Grace Feller?

She's right here and would like to ask you a few questions about it." He handed the cell to Lindsay and dug the key to the cuffs out of his pocket. He fit it into the lock and released them, while listening to her end of the conversation.

"Could you tell me everything she said? Please?" The strain in her voice was evident. She was silent as her hand was freed, listening intently. Then the color drained from her face with a suddenness that sent alarm spiking through him.

He frowned, reached to take the phone from her unresisting fingers. "Yeah, Darrell? I'm going to take lost time for a couple hours. I'll be in around ten." He disconnected the call, his attention focused on Lindsay.

She looked like she'd been sideswiped by a cement truck. And there was a dazed numbness to her expression that he didn't trust. Jack took both her hands in his and rubbed them gently. "What's wrong, baby? What'd he tell you?"

"What you said." The words were faint. Her eyes distant. "And that Mom told him she'd gotten a call. They never did get a TV." Her voice trailed off. "Plenty of work on a dairy farm, and what time's left is for homework and the Bible."

Because she looked like she could use the support, he slipped an arm around her shoulders and squeezed lightly. "That's not what has you looking like you saw a ghost. Who called her? A neighbor?"

"A man claiming to be a friend of mine. Said he'd been in contact with me here. Had shown me some of his engravings. And that he hoped to get a sample to them real soon."

"Son of a bitch." Jack could see the exact instant when the numbness wore off and left stark reality in its place. Lindsay's body sagged against him, as if folding in on itself. His other arm came up to cradle her close to his chest. But he was fresh out of comforting things to say.

Rassi's threat couldn't have been more obvious.

She shuddered against him, silent streams of tears tracing down her face. A vise squeezed inside his chest. Her soundless weeping carved at his insides, hollowing out his gut. A woman's tears always left him feeling helpless. Lindsay's made him feel like smashing something. Anything that would put her world right again.

"He's not going to win," he murmured, lips brushing her hair. Tightening his arms around her, he rocked her a little, calming them both. "We're aren't going to let the bastard win."

It might have been a minute. Could have been ten. But soon enough Lindsay straightened, strained against his hold. Jack dropped his arms, brushed at the dampness on her cheek with his thumb.

There was a terrible grimness to her eyes when she looked up at him. "I need to speak to your captain."

Lindsay didn't know what Jack had told Captain Telsom over the phone, but apparently it had been enough to convince the man to come here to interview her, instead of her going downtown. He'd said very little as she'd relayed her story, and it was impossible to get a read on him. Other than a few terse questions, some for her and others directed at Jack, he'd mostly listened. And now that she'd finished, she leaned back on the cushion of the couch, a sense of urgency taking root in her stomach.

"And you've got verification from NYPD on this guy?" The captain's statement was directed at Jack, who nodded.

"Right before you arrived I heard from ballistics. The bullets CSU recovered yesterday matched those taken out of eleven victims in the New York City area in the last five years. NYPD suspect Rassi is behind the hits at the direction of the Portino family there. But they've never gotten close to tying him to any of the homicides."

Telsom rubbed his jaw, then looked at Lindsay. "I suggest you call your family. Advise them to leave town for a while. Maybe stay with relatives."

Lindsay shook her head. "They won't go." She saw the look on both the men's faces, tried to explain. "My parents have livestock. Dairy cattle. I can only recall two times in my life when they both left the farm for more than a few hours at a time."

"You'll have to tell them what's been going on with you." Jack leaned forward, his hands clasped between his knees. "Once they understand the danger…"

A wistful smile curled her mouth as she thought of her family. Funny how the very things that drove her to rebellion as a teenager brought on a wave of nostalgia now. "They can't understand. They're simple people living a purposefully simple life. And this is completely outside their comprehension. If you could send the sheriff out there, he may be able to convince them." She hoped. "I don't want to call them unless it's from a secure phone. I'm afraid Niko might have had their phones tapped a long time ago, hoping to trace me through a call home." Certainly he'd known just how to flush her out, once he'd narrowed down her location.

She saw the look Telsom and Jack exchanged. Then the captain nodded. "All right. We'll reach out to law enforcement there. What county is your family in?" Lindsay told him and he pulled a notebook out of his suit jacket pocket, wrote it down. "The sheriff can send someone out there until we put the rest of the information together here."

Corroborated her story, he meant. The thought didn't bother Lindsay. But the time it was all going to take was beginning to burn. She had the sense that time was rapidly running out. "Do what you need to do. Niko Rassi is in Metro City. And I'm willing to deliver him to you."

Jack's gaze was sharp. But before he could say anything, Telsom spoke. "What do you have in mind?"

"He's here for me. Let's give him what he wants. Use me to draw him out."

"Are you out of your freaking mind?" Jack surged to his feet, fists clenched.

Telsom gave him a speculative look before returning his attention to her. "You want to play a part in his capture?"

"You won't catch him without me." An eerie sense of calmness had come over her. She knew exactly what she had to do. Funny how things simplified when options ran out. "You can take this opportunity to land a cold-blooded killer the NYPD has failed for years to build a case against. Or I can call the New York branch of the FBI and offer them the same deal." From the expression on both men's faces, she knew she'd hit a nerve. "Scooping up Rassi gives them a vital informant about the Portino family. Of course, I'd rather the MCPD got him. I don't want to chance him getting offered a deal from the feds and not paying for what he's done."

Although at this point it seemed like a luxury to still hope there would be justice for Niko Rassi. That he'd pay for the deaths of Ricky, Nathan and Wendy. But that didn't mean she'd stop fighting for it.

When the silence in the room stretched, she gave them a verbal nudge. "Would it clarify things if you saw the pictures on that memory card?"

"You said it was in New York."

Lindsay shot Jack a bland glance. "I lied." Rising, she crossed to the steps and returned to the spare bedroom, aware that Jack was behind her. She kneeled next to her suitcase and dumped it on the floor. Then she carefully removed the plastic strip providing support on the bottom. Not without difficulty, she withdrew it from the bag, turned it over. The memory card was wrapped inside a small velvet jewelry bag, taped to the bottom of the strip.

She pulled it free and handed it to Jack. He opened the bag and took out the card, looking from it to her. And his expression made her nervous in a way she could ill afford. "I couldn't tell you."

His dark stare had her stomach jittering. "You could have. You didn't." Turning his back, he walked back down the hall. Leaving her on her haunches beside the dismantled bag.

Slowly, she fit the plastic strip back inside the suitcase. Repacked her belongings, with more care than she'd originally taken. She wasn't going to feel regret for not being completely honest with Jack about the pictures. She'd survived this long by being cautious. And it wasn't as though his actions in the last twenty-four hours merited sainthood.

But he'd believed her without the proof she carried. Which equaled trust. A trust she hadn't completely reciprocated.

Lindsay shrugged impatiently, wishing she could slough off the sense of guilt as easily. Striding down the hall, she headed back to the living room. She'd had no reason in the last several years to offer unconditional faith to anyone. Certainly not the police.

Which made her ties to three cops in Metro City difficult to explain. And her growing feelings for Jack even more inexplicable.

When she re-entered the living room she found the two men huddled around Jack's computer, a digital camera plugged into it. She didn't want to look. Just the thought of seeing those images again had nausea stirring. Not knowing the victims didn't lessen the dreadfulness.

But like lead filings to a magnet, her gaze was pulled to the screen where the first picture had unfolded. Seeing Niko's satisfied smile again struck her with the force of a blow.

Oh God. She hauled in a breath, but her lungs still felt strangled. With a shaking hand she reached out, grabbed the back of Jack's chair for support. It was like being catapulted through time, to when Nathan and Ricky first had shown her the pictures. Reliving the horror as revulsion and shock had careened through her system. The realization that she'd fallen for a monster. Had slept with him. Shared with him. Unwittingly exposed her family and friends to danger. Because she'd never once suspected the vile darkness that lurked beneath Niko's veneer of glossy charm.

She turned away from the computer, made her way to the couch on wobbly knees and sank down on it. The low conversation between Jack and his captain faded to a background buzz. The full magnitude of her plans finally hit her. She'd have to face Niko again. Her stomach twisted in knots. And when that time came she couldn't allow these emotions to distract her from what needed to be done. It was her only chance to right so many wrongs. The only way to keep her family safe.

And maybe…just maybe…if this thing actually worked and she got out of it alive…maybe she could learn to forgive herself for not seeing the man for what he was before it was too late.

Jack's cell phone rang, and he pulled it from his pocket to answer it. A moment later he signed off, turning to look at Lindsay over his shoulder. "That was a buddy of mine. Rammed the ballistics tests through in a hurry and then got a definitive match comparing them to those in the database. The bullets shot at us yesterday were fired from the same gun as those dug out of eleven victims in New York."

After Jack's news the next hour passed in a blur. Captain Telsom had left, taking the memory card with him, and Jack had spent most of the intervening time on the phone. When he finished, he crossed to the couch where she still sat and dropped down beside her. "I just got verification that the sheriff's office in your family's county have checked on them. Everyone's safe."

The bolt of worry that had been tightening inside her for the last couple hours eased a fraction. "They need to convince them to get off the farm. Make arrangements to hide them somewhere they'll be safe until Niko's in custody." Would they be safe even then, she wondered? What if he got out on bail? All it would take was one phone call and he could have someone dispatched to Wisconsin to carry out his dirty work.

The thought strengthened her resolve. All the more reason to end it here. Now. To tie Niko up so tightly that he couldn't concentrate on anything other than his own survival. The fierce feeling of satisfaction at the thought couldn't be denied.

"Telsom will distribute a BOLO with copies of Rassi's likeness throughout the department. I've contacted security at the Metro City airport and they'll work on getting us the security tapes and passenger manifest. We gotta figure the possibility that he flew into LAX and rented a car. Getting the tapes and manifest from there will take longer. And going through the security tapes will take hours. But something will pop."

"He could have driven," she pointed out.

"Possible, but not probable." Jack settled deeper into the couch cushions, turned half toward her. "He would have had to see the first newscast. Recognized you immediately, without double-checking your likeness to positively ID you. I saw the newscast, remember. There were only fleeting glimpses of you. He would have had to take some time to be sure. Then he would have had to drive nonstop to get here." He lifted a shoulder. "Like I say, possible, but not very likely. But a gun nut like him probably would have preferred that."

"Gun nut?" She frowned. "I don't know about that. He kept a gun in the club, for intimidation in case of trouble, he said. Another in his apartment. But he didn't have a collection. He never even went shooting, that I knew of." Not for the first time, she was reminded that she hadn't known Rassi nearly as well as she'd thought.

"Ballistics paints a picture of a gun freak. He measures his own ammunition, or uses a reloader. It's a painstaking task and kinda pointless when you can buy the ammunition ready to go. Only the real fanatics get that into it, in my experience."

Lindsay mulled that over for a moment. "That might fit. He's very precise. Very exacting." The first time he'd ever struck her had been after she'd left an article of clothing lying on the floor of his apartment. His show of temper had shocked and frightened her. She'd left then, tried to break it off. But after a few weeks he'd wooed her back with flowers and apologies. The memory burned. She'd believed his excuses of stress and exhaustion. And he'd never hit her again. Until after the pictures surfaced.

Another thought occurred then. "What's a reloader look like?"

"I'll show you." She followed Jack to the computer and

he typed the word into a search engine. Studying the image he found, she shook her head. "I never saw anything like this."

"Like I say, not that many people bother with them."

"No, I mean, there was nothing like this in his office at the club. Not in his apartment or in the house he kept in the country." She thought for a moment. "Come to think of it, I never saw anything that could be used to engrave the shells, either."

Following her line of thought, Jack nodded. "So he's got a safe house. Probably an apartment somewhere in the city rented under an alias. Makes sense. Might be where he keeps his trophies, too, since he's the type to take souvenirs."

He swiveled in the computer chair to face her. "There'll be a half dozen officers here in a couple hours. I think— and the captain agrees—that this place is as safe for you as anywhere else we could come up with. So this becomes the site of operations before much longer." His eyes were unfathomable. "It isn't too late to change your mind."

"I'm not going to change my mind."

His gaze never wavered. "We'll minimize your exposure. Whatever the final plan entails, you won't be at risk. I'll make sure of that."

She wanted, badly, to reach out and lay a hand along his stubbled jaw. To stroke the grimness from his expression and remove the bleakness from his eyes. That he would try to reassure her, even knowing she'd never been completely honest with him, was almost more than she could bear. And she wished with all her might that she could have been a normal woman. Met him under regular circumstances.

Because the strength of that longing frightened her, she gave him a slight smile. "Well, if this is going to become cop central in a few hours, I think I'll take this time to get cleaned up." She turned and forced herself to head to the stairs. But before she'd ascended all the way something had her halting, before facing him again. "Lying to you about the memory card...that wasn't personal. Just reflex, you know?"

He gave a brief nod. "Sure."

"But I could have told you." She didn't miss the sudden stillness that came over him at her words. "I know I could have trusted you."

He said nothing. She didn't expect him to. But neither did she expect him to surge out of the chair, and cross the room toward her, his eyes blazing with an emotion that had her catching her breath. He reached her in a few long strides, and crowded her against the wall. Taking her face in both of his hands, he lowered his mouth to hers.

The first taste of him was combustible. Heat beckoned heat as her lips twisted beneath his. It was too easy to remember the last time they'd touched. And everything that had happened since then lent a feeling of urgency to the moment.

She parted her lips and his tongue swept in, certain and demanding. Threading her fingers through his hair, she pulled him closer, reveling in his urgency.

Their mouths battled, lips and teeth and tongue intent on a sensual journey all too easily recalled. Desire was already snapping through her veins, summoned effortlessly by this man. Recognizing that didn't alarm her as it once had. Exposing that streak of wildness inside was a pleasure when met and matched by his.

Jack moved closer, until she was pressed tightly between his body and the wall. And still it didn't seem close enough. One taste of her hadn't satisfied. His hunger for her had only been whetted. The urgency could have stemmed from the situation. The danger that still awaited.

He wished he could believe that.

Sliding his hand inside her loose T-shirt, he felt the smooth, satiny skin beneath and knew the truth. The coiling in his gut was due to this woman, Lindsay or Gracie or whatever she called herself. They matched, somehow, fire and fire, and he couldn't reason it away. Didn't want to.

Instead he wanted to feel the narrow length of her back. His palm swept up her spine. The delicate hollow between her shoulder blades. The baby-soft skin at the nape of her neck. And he wanted—needed—to forget everything else. To shove it aside and concentrate on only the two of them. To mate with her. To brand her so deeply, so intimately, she could never deny their connection. To steep himself in her until he was finally satiated.

He wondered dimly if that would ever be possible.

His hand passed over her stomach, where the muscles quivered beneath his touch, and then cupped her breast. He could feel his pulse churning, like a stallion straining at the scent of a favored mare. His response to her was too immediate. Too primal. But he didn't try to temper it.

He found her nipple and squeezed it lightly between his thumb and forefinger. Lindsay twisted against him, and he felt a flare deep in his gut. There was something viscerally satisfying in knowing that he didn't have to rein in the towering need rampaging inside him. That this woman could meet it, return it like two flames melding to burn even brighter. Knowing that drove him a little crazy.

Tearing his mouth from hers, he stripped the shirt off her, dispensed with the bra, and took a moment to look at her. Her nipples were already hard, turgid, begging for his lips. But he was the supplicant here. Lowering his mouth, he took one nipple between his teeth and batted it with his tongue. Lindsay wrapped one leg around his and pressed his head closer to her breast. Obeying her unspoken command, Jack stopped teasing her nipple to draw it more deeply into his mouth.

He suckled strongly from her, his free hand toying with her other breast, and felt her twist against him, her fingers clutching at his shoulders. Her touch was quick and frantic, and she wrestled with the buttons of his shirt, slipped her hands inside and skated them along his flesh to his shoulders. The slight sting of pain from her nails on his skin just fanned the flames hotter. Higher. And he knew he wasn't going to be able to make this last.

There was a thrumming in his ears, a tightness in his belly that signaled his dwindling control. It was too hot. Too fast. Too wild. But the need wouldn't be denied.

Raising his head, he hauled in a breath, a greedy gulp of air, hoping to calm his raging hormones. But he made the mistake of dragging his eyes open, looking at her. And his blood fired, sending a scorching bolt of lust through his belly.

Her torso was willow slender, her breasts smooth, white globes tipped with tightly knotted nipples. He'd never been one to get turned on by piercings, but damned if that tiny hoop in her navel wasn't amazingly sexy.

The pulse beat madly at the base of her throat, and he couldn't resist biting that sensitive skin lightly, like a man sampling a delicacy. It was a primitive need, the desire to taste flesh, to steep his senses in her. But it was a craving that couldn't be satisfied, no matter how he tried.

He nibbled along her jaw, attempting to rein in his rampaging lust. There was more of her to savor, to explore with lips and hands, teeth and tongue. Places he'd learned that made her gasp and sigh. Places he wanted to linger over again.

But he had the self-control of a sixteen-year-old in the backseat of his daddy's car. And if they didn't get to a bed soon, he was going take her with a similar lack of finesse.

Hooking an arm around her waist, he half carried her up the rest of the steps into the hallway. She gave a throaty chuckle at his hurry, and the sound torched his passion, a lit match to a gasoline-soaked fuse.

He halted, pressing her up against the wall. Their hands battled as she attempted to pull off his shirt. In the end he let go of her long enough to strip it off and toss it to the floor before crowding her against the wall again. Catching both her hands in his, he pinned them above her head and simply feasted on her.

He skated his lips over the curve of her shoulder. Dipped his tongue in the hollow above her collarbone. Her breasts were flattened against his chest, her nipples stabbing at him, and all he could think of was more. More time. More pleasure. More of her. Only of her.

A hot ball of need tightened in his belly. Desire fogged his brain. He let go of her to undo his jeans, drag them down and kick them away. Then froze when Lindsay hooked her thumbs in the sides of her pants and slowly rolled them down her hips.

Jack's mouth dried. In what had to be deliberate slowness, she inched the fabric down a fraction at a time, revealing a tiny scrap of black panties. When they finally made it down the length of those silky thighs she tugged them the rest of the way and stepped out of them. And the sight she presented did nothing to harness his restraint.

Breathing like a stevedore, he used his one last sliver of sanity. He retrieved a condom from his jeans with the intention of putting it on and carrying her to his bed. But she took it out of his hands and stepped closer to him, her eyes on his as she opened the wrapper and sheathed him, her movements as excruciatingly slow as her earlier strip-tease. His good intentions abruptly evaporated.

He hooked an arm around her waist and hauled her closer, his hands streaking over her skin, his touch just shy of des-perate. Sneaky little demons from hell were surging through his veins, calling to untamed instincts he usually quelled.

Moving her backward until the wall was at her shoul-ders, he caught the side of her panties with one finger and gave a tug, felt them come apart in his hand. He lifted her then, his only thought to have her. To bury himself so deeply inside her that it would be impossible to tell where he ended and she began.

Lindsay clasped her ankles around his waist and he nearly groaned aloud, sweat beading on his forehead. Her position opened her slick softness to him and he guided himself to her moist opening, his breathing ragged.

Her head lolled on her shoulders as he nudged her opening with the tip of his shaft; his muscles tightened as he battled back the savage urge to take her with one hard stroke.

Lindsay's back bowed as she slammed her hips against his, taking him partially inside her. With her action he was lost. He surged into her, every nerve in his body quivering at the possession. He closed his eyes, sensation crashing inside in a rollicking careen toward release. He was helpless to temper his movements as they strained together, his hips pistoning against hers in an effort to get closer. Deeper. Faster. Harder.

She buried her face in his neck, muffling a sob as she climaxed. Her inner walls clenched and released around him, the tiny pulsations working on him. Need clawed through him as he hammered into her, colors wheeling behind his eyelids. Abruptly he came, pleasure screaming through his system. And when he let himself fall, he thought of nothing but her.

Chapter 11

They made it to the bed. Eventually. And the second bout might have been more leisurely, but it was no less satisfying. Now Lindsay lay in Jack's arms, wondering distantly how much time they had before Jack's fellow officers began invading the place. She couldn't rouse herself enough to care.

"So you grew up on a dairy farm. Just like the song." Jack's voice was muffled, as his head was buried between her breasts. "You know. Eight maids a'milking. Always thought that was sorta sexy. I always picture eight hotties dressed up in those little French maid uniforms, right? Strolling off to milk the cows. And then maybe, I don't know, playing naked in the hayloft or something after."

"That's a truly touching Christmas sentiment," she said dryly, giving his hair a tug. "The reality was somewhat less picturesque. And certainly less pornographic."

He lifted his head to grin at her and her stomach gave a quick little flip. With that devilish smile he could thaw a polar ice cap. She'd only recently discovered she wasn't Eskimo material.

"Or maybe girls didn't have to help with chores where you grew up."

"Since there was just my sisters and me, yes, we helped." Somehow she thought stories of hooking cows up twice a day to the milking machine wouldn't match the vision he'd shared. There was nothing mildly romantic about the daily routine of feeding and watering cows and mucking out stalls. Or the late nights during calving seasons. The long days of vaccinations.

She'd detested the monotony. Strained against the rigid parameters of her parents' fundamentalist religious beliefs. But she hadn't run away. True, her mom and dad had vehemently opposed her plan to go to New York City with Wendy after graduating early, but they hadn't forbidden it. Perhaps they'd realized even then that she'd have gone anyway.

"Faith was six years younger than me. Hope was eight years younger."

"Grace, Faith and Hope. Your parents had high standards."

"Standards I rarely met." And that, she recognized, had been the real reason she'd left. "I was always doing something to disturb the status quo. Like flying Billy Simpson's underwear from the church steeple—don't ask. Falling asleep in church. Swiping the communion bread when Wendy and I made fondue... I was a trial to my parents." A trial and a puzzle they had no real interest in solving. Her sisters had presented no such problems. They'd gotten up when asked, did their chores without question and never begged to go to town to *do* something. See a movie. Hang out with friends. Anything but slowly suffocate on that farm.

And she'd wondered, in the years she'd been on the run, if that had changed. Faith would be nineteen. Had she spent her high school years arguing to join the swim team? Play volleyball? Date? Or was she content to accept the life her parents mapped out for her? A job with the farm-supply store in Ellison. College on a rigidly religious campus nearby.

Those were the questions that circled in Lindsay's mind like busy little ants on those nights when sleep was elusive. She'd gone to New York to experience life for the first time and, yes, to get away from her parents' strictures. And for the first time in her life she'd felt able to breathe. But she'd never meant to leave her family completely. Niko was responsible for cutting her off from them. Her choices had been made with their safety in mind, but all of them had suffered in the process.

As if he'd felt the change in her emotions, Jack slid an arm under her. When he rolled he brought her with him, situating her atop him. Jack smoothed a palm down the line of her back. "I've got a trak phone ordered. The officers will bring it when they show up. You can safely use that to contact your parents."

She nodded, oddly disoriented by the thought. It seemed strange to suddenly have that freedom. As if her world had skidded off its axis and suddenly been put right again.

But it really wouldn't be anywhere near right until Niko was no longer a threat. To her or to those she loved.

"We need to get moving." Despite his words, Jack didn't stir, except to continue that soothing stroking down her back. "Get cleaned up. Rebandage your head. We're going to get company in less than an hour, and then things will start hopping."

He looked up at her, his free hand pushing her hair back from her face to cup her cheek. "It'll all be over soon. The only thing we need from you at this point is information. You don't have to expose yourself to risk. I'll make sure your safety is the first consideration in whatever strategy we come up with."

And when she stared into those dark eyes the realization punched through her: she'd do whatever it took to keep this man safe, too. And something told her their plans were bound to be at cross-purposes.

With a little rearranging, his living room had been changed into a staging area. Captain Telsom, Tactical Commander Mendel, entry team leader Tom Nelson, Chief of detectives Gary Franks and Detectives Bruce Folsby, Rich Simmons and Lance Pruin were setting up whiteboards on easels, laying out legal pads and placing a tap on Jack's phone, just in case. Jack knew more tactical members would be in the area, as well as three plainclothes officers posted around the outside of his town house.

But it was tough for Jack to concentrate on organizing the chaos when he was supremely aware of Lindsay in the next room.

With the trak phone Simmons had brought in, she'd called her parents for the first time in over three years. He craned his neck, but all he could see of her was her back as she spoke in a corner of the kitchen. He tried to imagine not speaking to his mom or stepdad for that long and failed. Somehow it was easier to imagine not speaking to his older sister for a long period of time, as she was, in his estimation, a couple hormone levels shy of certifiable, but…he had a choice. They all lived right here in Metro City. He could talk to all of them anytime he wanted. Spend holidays with them. Drop in for dinner.

Lindsay effectively had to cut her family out of her life for thirty-eight months.

"Langley!"

His attention jerked to the captain, who was regarding him impatiently. "I asked if you have any tape."

"Sure." He went to his desk in the corner and pulled open a drawer. Through the window he could see the unmarked car sitting across the street and the plainsclothes detective inside. With all the evidence of the precautions being taken to protect Lindsay, he shouldn't have this knot in his gut. But he had a feeling it wouldn't ease up until this thing was over and they had Rassi in custody.

And Lindsay was safe, once and for all.

When he'd turned back to the captain to give him the roll of tape, Lindsay was rejoining them from the kitchen. He surveyed her critically. Her eyes were bright, but there was color in her cheeks that hadn't been there when the detectives had started filing in. He hoped that was a good sign.

He tossed the roll of tape to Telsom and continued past the man to Lindsay. In a low voice, he asked, "Everything all right?"

She drew in a shaky breath but nodded. "For now. It was so…difficult. Especially trying to explain enough to my parents so that they'd understand the need to leave the farm for a while without terrifying them."

"The county sheriff's office should have given them a rundown already."

"They did. My parents have no frame of reference. It's

hard for them to take it all in. But they agreed to go to my aunt's in Madison for a few days. Neighbors will take over the chores until they get back." Her expression determined, she added, "This needs to be resolved as soon as possible."

"It will be." Because he didn't trust himself not to reach for her, he tucked his hands in the pockets of his jeans. "But we can't rush this. Every last detail will be planned and replanned. If you're ready, I think we can begin."

Nodding, she walked past him and caught the captain's eye. Telsom straightened. "Ready, Ms. Bradford?"

"I am." Her gaze scanned the others in the room. "I'm not sure where you want me to start."

The other officers stopped what they were doing and made their way back to the center of the living room.

"I'd like everyone to hear for themselves the story you shared with me earlier this morning."

The only sign of stress she showed was the tightness with which Lindsay clutched at the back of the couch, where she remained standing. "My real name is Grace Feller. I've been running from a man named Niko Rassi for over three years."

The room was mostly quiet as she narrated the story she'd only told him in bits and pieces. Mostly under duress. Jack remained silent throughout until she came to the events of yesterday, and in quick, succinct words he revealed what they'd learned about the shooter since.

When they were finished, Captain Telsom stood up and passed out some folders. "I've been in contact with NYPD. These are files on the information we've been able to put together on Rassi." He gave the men a few minutes to flip through the information in them before continuing. "This guy's a professional. And if New York's right on this, he's had a lot of practice. We have to be careful, and we can't make mistakes. We may only get one chance at him."

He looked at Lindsay. "Ms. Bradford…Feller…has kindly offered her help in drawing Rassi out. We can conclude he came here for her, and since he missed the first time, he's going to be anxious for another chance."

"I suggest you let me contact him." Lindsay had the attention of every man in the room. She looked a bit frail but determined, Jack decided critically. She'd changed into jeans and a tank top beneath an unbuttoned short-sleeve navy blouse. The stark white bandage was partially visible through her hair, and the adjective he'd verbalized after she went home from the hospital sprang to mind again. She looked tragic. But he understood her objection to the term. Because despite what had befallen her, she was nobody's victim. She wasn't cowed. He was the only man in the room who understood just how strong she really was.

"I can use the trak phone to call his New York number. He'll be checking his messages. He has a business there to run and I imagine he wouldn't risk missing a communication from the Portinos. I'll leave the number of this phone. He'll call back." The fleeting flicker of expression across her face was difficult for Jack to identify. "I'm sure of that."

"I'm thinking we can arrange a meet between the two of them," Jack put in. "He'll expect her to be afraid. He's threatened her family and tried to kill her. But Lindsay still has something Rassi wants so he'll also expect her to negotiate. We could pick a spot, public enough for her, deserted enough to satisfy him." He looked at Commander Mendel. "Can we get a decoy officer to stand in for her?"

The commander wasn't given a chance to respond. "That wasn't the deal." Lindsay's voice was sharp. "*I* go. This isn't some dumb guy off the street you're dealing with like Mitch Engels. There's a reason Rassi hasn't been caught. He'll have some sort of strategy in place to verify my identity before he ever gets anywhere near the meeting place. If something's off, he'll know it, and you'll blow your chance at him. And my family will still be in danger."

That knot in Jack's belly tightened. He glanced at Mendel. "It's an unnecessary risk. She can fully brief the decoy on any personal information Rassi might bring up to test her identity. Or we can wire the female cop and Lindsay can feed her any answers she might need. There are multiple ways to go about this that don't involve placing her in Rassi's sights."

"It's my choice—"

"The hell it is." He knew the other men were looking at him speculatively, but there was a fear growing inside him that wouldn't let him back off. She couldn't understand how quickly situations like these could go to hell, no matter how well they were planned. And if it went south, she'd be grabbed by Rassi or she'd be dead. Just the thought had a cold sweat beading on his forehead.

With effort, he managed a steady tone as he addressed both Telsom and Mendel. "A trained professional in that position is best for everyone. She'd react quicker, for one thing. She'd think like a cop, which would be a huge bonus in a situation like this."

"The original deal still holds," Lindsay interjected. "We do this with my full involvement or I make the same offer to the feds."

"Why don't we all calm down and we'll start dealing with the details," Telsom suggested mildly. "I'm going to get a water. Anyone else want one?"

There was a chorus of yeses, so he walked in the direction of the kitchen, saying as he passed Jack, "Langley, why don't you help me serve these bums?"

He had no choice but to fall in behind the captain. When they got in the kitchen and out of sight of the other men, however, the other man turned on him, a steely look in his eye. "What's going on with you, Langley?"

Jack set his jaw. "Nothing. I'm stating my opinion."

"I got that. What I don't get is whether it's an objective one."

Stepping carefully in the verbal quicksand, Jack replied, "You know I'm right. There's no reason to use a civilian when a cop can do the job better."

Telsom was getting testier. "Ordinarily, but since her cooperation hinges on her involvement, in this case we use the civilian. She'll have SWAT coverage. She'll be safe enough. What I need to know is, do you have any personal interest here?"

The conversation had just gotten trickier. Jack met Telsom's gaze and lied. "My interest and my opinions are strictly professional." Any other answer would have gotten him bounced from the case, and there was no way he was chancing that.

Looking unconvinced, Telsom said, "Good. Then we don't have a problem, do we?"

Clenching his jaw, Jack shook his head. He yanked open the refrigerator with barely restrained violence and started withdrawing the bottled water the detectives had brought in. He had a problem with this, all right. But the play was predetermined, and if he wanted in the game he'd keep his mouth shut and follow orders. Because their biggest challenge wasn't letting Lindsay face down Niko Rassi again.

It was keeping her alive while she did it.

Lindsay didn't take more than a couple bites from her pizza before her stomach rebelled. She replaced it on her plate and reached for her water instead. By the growing mound of empty pizza boxes, the detectives situated around the room didn't share her queasiness.

Jack was having no trouble eating. If she'd counted correctly he was on his third piece and good-naturedly arguing with the man next to him over his next slice.

She wondered if she was the only one who could see through his easygoing surface to the temper simmering beneath.

Perhaps, since the temper was directed at her, she was the only one aware of it. And she sorely wished everyone else in the room could disappear for ten minutes so she and Jack could just have it out and get it over with.

Not that discussions had ever proved particularly fruitful where he was involved. She set the water down on the counter with a little more force than was necessary. He seemed to think handcuffs and petty larceny passed for a mature exchange of opinions. And all the discussion in the world couldn't change the fact that they'd never agree on this issue.

She picked at the corner of the bottle's label with her thumbnail. How could he understand how terrified she was at the idea of seeing Rassi again? But that emotion was nothing compared to the thought of sitting safely in Jack's apartment hoping things went well with the meeting they set up. And the mountain of guilt she'd suffer if the plan went awry and someone else paid with their life.

Just the thought filled her with a sick pool of dread. In the grand scheme of things, she had far more important things to concentrate on than Jack's mood.

Like the message she'd left on Niko's machine.

It had been simple enough to record after the robotic voice's invitation. Not like talking to the man at all. And she'd been carefully coached by the detectives on what to say. How to sound. They'd walked her through every step of the conversation she'd have with him when he returned her call.

But it was the waiting for the call that was excruciating. And somehow she knew that was exactly the way Niko had planned it.

Lindsay dreamed of Wisconsin. The rolling green hills punctuated with trees. The acres of pasture surrounding the farm, dotted with black-and-white cows. The trim, old-fashioned barn, freshly painted. Gravel roads ribboning through the countryside. Postcard perfect.

But shadows moved over the scene. A pulsing, breathing menace that punctured the peace. The roads swelled. Darkened. She saw them froth and bubble, angry rivers of blood slashing through the hills. Covering the livestock. The grass. The buildings. It rose and built until it carried away everything that belonged there. She saw her family swimming feebly against the tide of it, and screamed silently. Struggled to reach them. But she couldn't move. The wall of blood held her stationary even as it carried away everything she cared about. And all she could do was struggle and scream and scream and scream...

She woke with a gasp, sitting upright in bed, her breath heaving out of her lungs as if she'd uttered those screams that had been trapped inside her. Swiping a hand over her face, she discovered her cheeks were damp. It had seemed so real...

The cell phone next to her bed shrilled and her attention jerked toward it. That's what had awakened her. Pulled her from one nightmare into the real thing.

"Wait."

Jack was standing in the doorway, wearing only a pair of hastily donned jeans that he hadn't bothered to fasten. As the cell rang again he flipped on the hallway light and called downstairs. "You ready?"

"Give me a minute," came a disembodied voice. Then after the next ring, "Okay. Go."

Lindsay reached for the trak phone and brought it to her ear. "Hello?" It wasn't an effort to manufacture the groggy tone. But it took every bit of strength she had not to recoil when she heard the voice on the other end.

"Gracie. We have unfinished business, you and I."

Jack crossed the room to sit down beside her, tilting his head close to hers to hear what he could of the other side of the conversation.

"Seems to me you tried to finish that business a couple days ago."

"I might have been a bit overzealous. Jet-lagged, you know. But if I'd wanted you dead, you'd be in the ground."

"I appreciate your restraint."

His low laugh had a chill breaking out over her skin. "Ah, Gracie. I've missed you, you know. Tell me, who was that with you at your apartment? Someone you're screwing?"

"If you wanted an update on my love life, Niko, you came a long way for nothing." She was supremely aware of the detectives listening in on the conversation downstairs. "I don't have one."

"We can change that. Although I can't say that I care for that dye job you've done." Incredibly, a tinge of possessiveness entered his tone. "You knew how much I loved your hair. Why'd you cut it?"

Jack was signaling her to draw out the conversation. But God help her, she didn't know how much longer she could without retching. The sound of his voice had never faded from her memory. To hear it live filled her with revulsion.

Not to mention fear. A sharp, cold blade of it was slicing through her, leaving her feeling shredded and vulnerable. And that was precisely his intention.

"As I said in my message, I think it's time we put an end to our disagreement. We need to come to a compromise."

His laugh sounded again, ugly and satisfied. "You're hardly in a position to bargain. How is that family of yours, anyway? I'll bet your sister is getting to that sweet age. Ripe for the plucking. Maybe I should forget all about you and have her brought to me. I could teach her everything I taught you."

Her stomach twisted in silent protest. "We both know you aren't interested in my family. Or in me. But you are interested in that memory card."

There was a pause. When he spoke again the bantering tone was gone and his words were laced with menace. "You have cost me time and money, bitch, and my patience is nearly gone."

"I didn't know you had any. Patience, that is."

Jack was violently shaking his head, and she could read his lips: *Don't bait him!*

But there was a strange calm coming over her. She'd never backed down from Niko when they were together. Not until the end. Not until she'd learned what he was capable of. He wouldn't expect her to play it timid and meek. She was following her instincts on this one.

"I indulged you too much when we were together. You needed more discipline."

"I've learned discipline, Niko. I've learned how to get what I want. You can have what you want, too. The memory card in exchange for your promise to leave my family alone."

"You'll have made copies of the photos."

"And that's incentive for you to keep your promise." She held her breath, prayed he'd dig no further. She'd been a naive innocent when she was with him. And it'd take an innocent to believe she could bargain with the likes of him. She just needed him to believe she was the same woman he'd known years ago.

"Tell me where you're at. I'll pick you up."

It was one thing, Lindsay thought, to want him to think her naive. It was another to have him believe she was stupid. "I think not. We'll meet in the daylight. A public place." She pretended to think for a moment. "There's a Metrodome on Interstate 57. It's closed for repairs. Meet me in the south parking lot at noon tomorrow."

"Nine-thirty. And I'm sure I don't have to remind you what happens if you involve the cops."

A boulder-size lump formed in her throat. Going to the cops in New York had signed her friends' death warrants. "That didn't work out particularly well last time."

"For either of us. The detective cost me a good sum before he met…an unfortunate accident. And his death is on your head. For bringing him into it. If you make that mistake again, your family is dead."

She had to force the word out. "Understood."

"Good." His tone turned oily as he said caressingly, "And, Gracie? Wear something sexy for me. We have some catching up to do."

Jack caught the phone when she would have dropped it, and she leaned forward, her head between her knees. Her stomach heaved and roiled and it was all she could do to avoid being sick.

"Tell me you got something," he called to the crew downstairs.

There were voices raised in response but she couldn't make them out. There was a buzzing in her ears, a pounding in her chest. She hauled in great gulps of air, battling back the wave of emotion that churned and whipped inside her.

"It's not too late." Jack's voice in her ear was urgent. "There's another way to do this. You don't have to be at the meet. Why put yourself through it? There's no point."

It was a long moment before she was able to straighten again. Longer before she could manage a response. "I don't expect you to understand. But I *do* have to go through with this." She owed it to her friends. To Nathan. Ricky. Wendy. All of them lay cold and buried because she'd brought Niko Rassi into their lives. He was still a threat. He'd be a threat until he was behind bars.

Feeling ancient, she rose and went to join the detectives downstairs. It was seven hours before she would meet with Niko again.

Sleep would be impossible.

Niko Rassi pulled the rental car back into the slot in front of his motel room and got out of the vehicle. The stolen cell phone was now lying in the bottom of a storm sewer. He re-entered the room with a grimace of distaste. The place was a hellhole. But it accepted cash and the man at the front desk was suitably apathetic. From the looks of him, that apathy was chemically induced, which could only work in Niko's favor. His memory wasn't likely to be too reliable about the man who'd requested the cabin farthest from the road.

He locked the door behind him, smiled when he saw his

equipment lying neatly in wait for his return. Anticipation thrummed inside him, the buzz almost sexual.

Or maybe that reaction was the result of talking to Gracie again. Hearing her voice. God, she'd always been a smart-ass. Daring to talk to him the way no one else would. His fault, for allowing it. It had been necessary, of course, to bind her to him. She'd learned whom she was dealing with at the end.

He sat down at the rickety desk and reached into the box of shells. Each had been meticulously fed through his hydraulic reloader, packed with his signature load. But it was the top one he withdrew. One with the engraving he'd specially designed prior to loading it.

Gracie. One finger stroked the engraved lettering like a lover smoothing over bare skin. She'd pay for talking to him like that. She'd pay for many things. It had been necessary to make her think that she actually had a say in their meeting. That he didn't have every detail planned. But she'd learn that soon enough.

There was no hurry when he took her. Things in New York were calm for once. He could spare a few more days away, especially when he was so close to having everything he'd wanted for the last few years.

He'd told her the truth—she'd cost him dearly. And she'd pay for that. He'd take his time when he hurt her, fully enjoy the pleasure it brought him. She'd tell him exactly where those copies that she'd made of the photos were.

He got aroused just thinking about it. He took his gun out and laid it on the desktop, ejecting the cartridge to refill it with his chosen shells. He and Gracie had a lot of catching up to do. Just thinking of her creamy white skin and long, strong legs turned him rock hard. He'd screw her a few more times, just to see if it was as good as his memory recalled.

And this time when he was done with her, the bullet with her name on it would finally find its target.

Chapter 12

"Okay, you're miked for sound. I'll be the one walking you through it. Just remember the drill."

Lindsay nodded, though at the moment her mind was such a jumble that she couldn't have plucked out any one piece of information that had been drummed into her over the last few hours. Jack finished securing her bulletproof vest over the thin tank she wore. Then she slipped into the zippered sweatshirt someone had rounded up for her. Her own clothes wouldn't have fit over the vest.

"We'll have snipers situated on top of the Metrodome. Ava Carter will be up there, and she's the best. The construction trucks that have been present daily since the explosion will be there, but they'll be full of SWAT team members. No civilians will be on-site. Anyone you happen to see dressed as a construction worker is going to be one of us. Full perimeter will be secured around the area. Rassi's photo has been distributed."

She struggled with the zipper, her fingers feeling thick and wooden. "How will you keep other civilians from stumbling onto the scene without scaring off Niko?"

"Don't worry about that. It's what we do, okay?" Jack batted her hands aside and zipped the sweatshirt for her. "Tactical command and marksmen were set up before daylight. Some of the squad's already waiting in the construction vans parked there. The rest of us will arrive there by eight in other trucks supplied by the construction firm. To Rassi, everything's going to look normal."

Lindsay didn't dispute him, although doubt rolled queasily through her. Jack was probably right. He'd once told her she attributed too much power to Niko. He was evil but not omnipotent. And he was no match for a full SWAT team. She'd be safe enough.

The nerves churning in her stomach had much more to do with facing him again.

Jack surveyed her, his expression grim. "I hate this."

"You've mentioned."

If anything, his mouth went tighter. "It's not too late. No one would blame you for deciding to allow a decoy—" When she shook her head, he broke off, then cursed.

"I'm the one who will draw him there. He recognized me from a few seconds on the news, Jack. He's not going to be fooled by a random decoy." He wouldn't understand that she needed to do this. Needed to face down the monster who'd murdered her friends. Terrorized her. Threatened her family. It had all started with her and Niko. It had to end that way, too.

"Langley!"

Telsom's bellow up the steps had Jack grimacing. "I've got to go."

There was a tug in her heart, a quick little squeeze. "I know. Be careful."

A muscle jumped in his jaw, but he only gave her a curt nod and strode out the door. Lindsay released a shaky breath, prepared to follow him. But he reappeared as quickly as he'd exited.

"What—"

He didn't give her time to complete the question. He was at her side in two quick steps, one arm hauling her to him. And his mouth covered hers, all his pent-up frustration rife in his kiss.

His lips were hard, demanding. And she returned the demand with her own. The familiar thrill zinged through her system, awakening a thousand nerve endings already spiked with adrenaline. There was just time to lock her arms around his neck. To go on tiptoe and twist her mouth beneath his, drawing as much as she could of the taste and texture of his lips before he broke away again. And the intensity of his gaze was fierce enough to torch her blood.

"Don't do anything stupid."

The utter lack of sentiment in his words was belied by the heat in his eyes. "You, either."

And this time when he walked out the door, she knew he wouldn't be back. She sank down on the bed. Took a deep, calming breath. And then meticulously went over every detail the detectives had drummed into her. In less than two hours she was going to see Niko again. Talk to him. And maybe this time, finally, he was going to account for everything he'd cost her.

The vest was hot. Coupled with the sweatshirt, it was boosting Lindsay's body temperature by several degrees.

She could feel perspiration trickling down her back as she sat in the car in the south lot of the Metrodome.

Time inched by at snail speed. Mendel had decreed that she arrive twenty minutes early. He'd said, and she agreed, that it would seem normal for her to try and arrive first. Niko wouldn't approach unless he saw her, anyway.

"Okay, it's nine-twenty. You can get out of the car." Jack's voice sounded in the earbud microphone she wore, hidden by her hair. She knew he'd be relaying orders from the commander. His voice would be the only one she heard throughout the incident, and there was comfort in that. She wasn't alone. Not this time.

She left Detective Simmons in position, crouched down in the back floor of the car, and got out of the vehicle. Threw a quick anxious look around the area that wasn't totally pretense.

"Okay, that's good. Look a little jittery, he'd expect that. Walk out to the center of the lot and stop. Look around some more."

She did as he directed. The lot was practically empty. Telsom had made sure the Metrodome management and construction crew stayed away. So the men she saw scattered on the scaffolding with piles of brick and mortar had to be cops.

Shielding her eyes with her hand, she looked down the long drive running past the lot. It was a designated drive, so any car on it would have to be purposefully approaching the Metrodome. There was no other destination.

Turning to pace, she scanned the area. If she had come here alone, she might have found the presence of the "workers" mildly comforting. If she hadn't known just what Niko was capable of.

"We've got a car turning into the drive."

Her stomach lurched. She managed to turn and pace, as if impatience and nerves required a release. That wasn't far from the truth.

"Posted officers will be checking ID. Hang on. You're doing great."

Despite the dispassionate professional tone—or perhaps because of it—Lindsay found Jack's voice in her ear calming. Reassuring. She could have done this without him. Would have. But she couldn't deny that knowing he was close made it easier. And now wasn't the time to examine the reasons for that.

In the distance she could see an inflatable Santa gently bobbing in front of a store. The incongruity of the sight filled her with dark humor. If all went according to plan, Niko would spend Christmas behind bars. But somehow the thought failed to calm her.

Shoving her hands in the pocket of the sweatshirt, she continued to move. It was past time for the meeting. Nine-forty the last time she checked. But yeah, it would be like Niko to keep her waiting. To make sure she was crawling out of her skin with nerves before he made an appearance.

"Indefinite ID. We're going to allow the car to enter the lot. Stay well clear of it. Move in front of the construction van with the ladder on top."

With her pulse pounding in her ears, Lindsay obeyed. The directive would give her cover in case Niko was in the car and intent on a drive-by shooting. But she knew instinctively he wasn't going to risk that. There was the memory card, for one thing. He would want to have possession of that before he dispensed with her.

And his ego would demand doing this face-to-face. He'd want to see her fear. He'd delight in watching her reaction when he taunted her with threats. She could appreciate the emotion. There was a part of her that would be deeply satisfied at watching *his* reaction when the place swarmed with cops.

The car cruised by, to pull up close to the structure. Time stilled. Her lungs burned. Lindsay hadn't even realized she'd been holding her breath. The car door began to swing open. A figure emerged.

Her breath whooshed out of her. Unless the intervening time had been very unkind to him, the car's occupant wasn't Niko. This man was short, stout and balding, with an ill-tempered expression that heralded ire.

"Hey, you! Where's your boss?"

Lindsay eyed the man carefully, but he wasn't paying any attention to her. His gaze was fixed on one of the "workers" on the scaffolding.

"Foreman should be here soon." Staying in character, the responding officer continued to slap bricks on the exterior of the structure.

"I don't care about your damn foreman. I'm talking about Patten, the owner."

"He doesn't show up on-site often. I wouldn't expect today to be any different."

"Well, apparently he doesn't show up at his office, either, since he doesn't return my phone calls. Where can I find him?"

"Stay where you are," Jack advised through the mic. "We don't have a clear view into his vehicle."

After a few more minutes it was clear, at least to her, that the stranger was no more than another client of the construction company's, and a disgruntled one at that. After several minutes of shouting at the "worker" on the scaffolding, he got back into his car and squealed away, turning toward the exit.

"Okay, false alarm." Jack's voice held a note of humor. "It's nine-forty-five. Let's get back in place."

Feeling as though she were baking in the heavy body armor, Lindsay moved back out into the center of the lot. Another forty minutes crawled by, but no one else approached the parking lot.

Niko wasn't coming.

"Okay, he's a game player, you say." Telsom's visage was grim. "Maybe this is a ploy to throw you off stride. In that case he has to believe you'll contact him again."

"It's possible." Lindsay leaned against the car she'd driven there, emotionally drained. The adrenaline high had seeped out of her with a suddenness that left her legs feeling like water. "He'd want me to know who was calling the shots. He wouldn't have liked me making demands."

"So he'll try again." The captain's ruddy face was damp. "Langley will take you back to his place. We'll convene again in a couple hours and discuss our next move." Almost as an afterthought, he added, "That all right with you, Ms. Feller?"

She nodded, and he walked briskly away. Seeing Jack heading her way, she rounded the car to allow him to drive. That would free her to get out of this vest before it suffocated her. She didn't know how the officers could stand wearing it with its additional weight.

Jack got in and adjusted the seat while she divested herself of the sweatshirt. "You did great today."

"Lot of good it did us." She felt like one giant knot of nerves, and that, dammit, was probably exactly what Niko had intended. To keep her off guard and anxious. Easier to manipulate.

As Jack pulled out of the lot, she struggled out of the vest. The tactics would have worked on the woman Niko had known three years ago, she admitted silently. But the life she'd lived since had hardened her in ways he could never imagine.

"There will be another contact. He can't afford to waste a lot of time. He's got a business back in New York City, right? He isn't going to want to spend a lot of time away from it. He's jerking you around, trying to keep you off balance."

"So what's the next step?"

"Telsom's calling the shots there." Jack checked his mirrors before changing lanes. "I'm guessing once you talk to Rassi again, he's going to set the time and place. Show you who's running the show. So we'll have to get a list of possible sites you'll agree to and arrange the same sort of scene all over again. Different date and time."

Lindsay leaned forward and flipped the controls to the air-conditioner to full blast. Even the tepid air flowing from the vents felt cool to her heated skin. "I want it over," she muttered, leaning her head back against the headrest. One way or another, she wanted to be free to go on with her life. Whatever that might entail. Things really hadn't changed at all. Just like the last thirty-eight months of her life, Niko Rassi was still calling the shots.

"I'm going up to grab a shower."

While Lindsay entered the house ahead of him, Jack turned to check the car parked across the street. He could make out the figure of the officer behind the wheel. It was tedious and boring work, but he was glad Telsom had insisted on keeping the surveillance team in place.

Entering the town house, he locked the door behind him and crossed to the kitchen. Although a cold beer would taste damn good right now, he'd have to settle for water, since he was on duty. He withdrew two bottles from the refrigerator and went to the stairs, calling, "You want a bottle of water?"

Her muffled response could have meant anything, so he trotted up the steps to her room. "I'm also quite helpful in the shower capacity, if you're—" He came to a halt in her doorway, the rest of the sentence freezing on his tongue.

Niko Rassi stood behind Lindsay, his arm wrapped around her throat, his hand clapped over her mouth. He wore an MCPD uniform.

And he had a gun pressed against her temple.

"A cop, Gracie?" He jammed the weapon harder against her skin. "You crawled in bed with a cop? My disappointment with you continues to mount." To Jack he said, "You'll want to take that weapon out of your harness there, Detective. Two fingers."

Slowly, Jack did as he was told, his mind racing. He hadn't been completely through the house, but Rassi must have come in the back. Which didn't explain how the hell he'd gotten by the surveillance team. But with dread pooling in the pit of his stomach, he had a suspicion.

"Good. Now toss it on the bed." When Jack did so, he walked Lindsay over a few feet, let go of her to reach for the gun and thrust it into his waistband. "Now let's see you lift your pant legs. I'm going to need your secondary weapon, as well, Detective. Let's not play games."

"Looks like you were a step ahead of us all the way," Jack said conversationally, taking his time withdrawing the second weapon. After one quick glance at Lindsay he kept his gaze firmly trained on Rassi. The desolation in her eyes was like taking a blade through the chest.

"It could have been played a number of ways, but it never pays to underestimate a beat reporter's hunger for a headline." Smugness sounded in his voice. "All it took was a call to the local rag. Convince the reporter on the cop beat that he had a chance to share a byline on CNN, and…" He lifted a shoulder. "His source discovered where *Ms. Bradford* was staying. Leaks. Departments are all full of them."

The roaring in his ears was playing hell with his thought processes. "He get you that uniform, too?" The shirt was a little tight, he noted. The pants a couple inches too short.

"This? Courtesy of the officer on duty in the car out back. He won't be needing it anymore. Now." He tapped the muzzle of the gun against Lindsay's skull. "I believe Gracie has something of mine she needs to return before she and I leave here."

"I gave it to you." Lindsay's voice was steady as she looked at Jack. "For safekeeping, the first night I was here. Remember?"

She hadn't given him anything that night, he recalled, but he'd taken a couple things. And hidden the gun and the money so she couldn't take off. "I remember. It's in my room." He made as if to move. "I'll just go and—"

"Don't be stupid. Keep your hands where I can see them and we'll all go together."

Jack headed toward his bedroom, with Rassi pushing Lindsay after him. "Kneel down at the foot of the bed," Rassi ordered him. "Hands behind your head."

A hundred plans ran through Jack's mind. None rated above desperate. He knew what Lindsay was planning, but he'd ejected the cartridge from her gun. Stashed them in two different places. There was no way she was going to be able to get to both of them and load the gun to use it on Rassi. "I know I put it in the closet. But damned if I can recall if I put it on the top shelf or in the toe of my black boot."

"Don't jerk me around, Detective. You're expendable, remember?"

Hands still on his head, he turned to look at the other man. "The hell of it is, I can't remember. Got a head injury in the Metrodome explosion a few months back and my short-term memory is crap."

Rassi studied him carefully, then gave Lindsay a push. "Look for it."

Intent on a diversion, Jack turned to face him as the man moved to keep Lindsay in his sights. "Maybe you and I can work something out."

With an ugly laugh, the other man said, "You cops are all the same. Always looking for the payoff."

From the corner of his eye, Jack could see Lindsay on all fours, his boot in her hand. "And why the hell shouldn't I be? Know what I got from my department after my injury? Ten percent of the medical bills, that's what I got. These memory lapses might be permanent, the doctor says. Get injured in the line of duty and what do I get to show for it?"

"It's not here," Lindsay reported.

"Then pull that chair over and get your ass up to check the shelf." Rassi narrowed a look at Jack. "You better not be jerking me around."

"I can help you here." Did Lindsay have the clip? He had to believe she did. Had to hope that she had some sort of familiarity with the gun he'd taken out of her bag and could load it quickly and silently. Because their options were pretty dismal, otherwise. "The way I figure it, you're going to need help getting out of town. Your picture's all over the department. Been distributed to the airports."

"Has it now?" A small smile crossed Rassi's lips. But his attention was focused on Jack, just as he'd planned. "Thanks for the tip. Guess I won't be using that return flight after all."

"I can arrange for a clean car. Flawless ID. A place to stay that will keep you out of the public eye until then."

"And all for the low price of…" Rassi's voice was bitter. "What do you California cops go for? Because the ones in New York are greedy bastards."

"We can work that out."

"Frankly, Detective, I don't need you."

"Actually, you do. I can tell you what's waiting for you in New York." And it was his turn to look smug at the arrested expression on Rassi's face. "See, we matched the ballistics on the slugs you fired and the shell you left behind to some unsolved homicides in New York. Now, once we get through the security films from the nearby airports— you flew here, right?—we've placed you here at the time of the shooting."

He'd given Rassi something to think about. He could tell from the expression on the man's face. But before he could say anything else, Lindsay said, "I found it."

There was a fraction-of-a-second opportunity when Rassi's attention shifted to her. Jack didn't waste it. He dove at the man's knees in a low tackle, knocking him off balance.

Rassi cursed, stumbled and fired. The shot came so close Jack could feel the heat of the bullet kissing his cheek. And the two of them crashed to the floor, rolled. Grappled for the gun. Jack sent a fist into Rassi's face, felt the satisfying crunch of bone on bone. The other man flailed beneath him, half turning over, but Jack continued landing blow after blow, all the pent-up fury at the man embodied in each hit. Everything he'd cost Lindsay. All the loss. The terror. Every minute of anguish he was going to pay for if Jack had to pound it from him one fist at a time.

Until Rassi rolled again to face him, this time with the weapon pointed directly at his face. Jack scrambled to his feet, inching away. Watched the man's finger tighten on the trigger.

"You're going to want to rethink that, Niko."

Jack saw Lindsay circling toward them, gun held in both hands. Slightly shaky hands, he noted sickly, but her expression was determined. "Put the gun down. Slowly."

Rassi looked from Jack to Lindsay. "He's a dead man before you fire a shot. And then you're next."

"You can't get off two shots before I put one in your brain. That's how you work, right? One shot center of the forehead. Doesn't take a whole lot of skill from this distance. But your job doesn't rely on skill, does it? It just takes a soulless, gutless coward." Her voice was filled with loathing. "Drop the gun."

Because he never took his eyes off Rassi, Jack saw the man's intent in his expression before he moved. With blinding speed he turned the gun on Lindsay.

"Watch out!"

The shot sounded before Jack had gone more than two steps toward her. For one panic-stricken second he froze, half expecting to see her crumple before him.

Comprehension followed an instant later as he swung toward Rassi. And saw the crimson blooming in the center of Rassi's shirt. Carefully, Jack stepped over his body to take the gun from his hand. "Call 911."

But Lindsay wasn't—big surprise—following orders. She came closer, weapon lowered but still chambered, to stare down at Rassi. Jack checked the man's vitals, grabbed a pillow from the bed to stanch the flow of blood.

"That's a kick, isn't it?" Rassi's gaze was on Lindsay, his words slurred. "Innocent little Gracie. In the end, you're no different than I am."

"You're wrong." Jack heard the thickness in her voice.

"If I were like you I'd put another bullet in you and end your miserable life. I prefer to think of you spending the rest of your days playing 'hide the soap' in the prison shower."

Her whole body trembled then, and Jack knew the shock was just hitting her. "Lindsay." He kept his voice gentle. "If you want to see him live long enough to wind up bunk buddies with a three-hundred-pound hillbilly named Bubba, you need to make that call."

Keeping the pressure steady on the wound, he gave Rassi a sardonic grin. "Personally, I could be convinced either way."

"Well, that should be all." Captain Telsom flipped his notebook closed and rose to signal the rest of the team. "CSU's done here and I think we are, too. Detective Langley can bring you down later for a formal statement." He shot a look at Jack. "Maybe you both ought to be checked out by the ER first."

"No!"

"That's not necessary." Their protests came simultaneously, but after a look from Jack, Lindsay subsided. "I would like to give…Ms. Feller the opportunity to rest before bringing her in. This whole thing has been a shock to her system. She's bound to crash soon."

"*She* is standing right here and perfectly capable of speaking for herself." Lindsay shot Jack a withering glare before addressing the captain. "I'll be down shortly."

"We've got what we need for now, but don't take too long. With Christmas in a couple of days, things at the station will be crazier than usual." His glance at Lindsay was accompanied by a slight smile. "I image you'll want to spend the holiday in Wisconsin."

Stunned, Lindsay watched him follow the officers out

the door. She was free to visit her family. To spend Christmas with them. Joy filled her.

She turned to Jack then, and another thought occurred. "Any chance of getting my gun back?"

His incredulous look was its own response. "I don't think I'd push it. Under the circumstances, we're going to have to do a fast shimmy to avoid charges. Carrying concealed. No permit. Best not to mention it at all to the captain."

She felt like kicking something. "That cost me a month's worth of tips at Joe's Coffee Stop."

"I can imagine."

It was amazing sometimes, she thought, inwardly squirming, how much he could look like a *cop*.

"Bought it for cash out of the trunk of a car in a back alley from some guy named Bruno?"

Because that was closer to the truth than she wanted to admit, she merely sniffed. "His name was Lenny."

His smile held a sharklike quality. "Even worse. So no. The gun is gone. Get used to it."

She supposed, in the great scheme of things, the weapon was of little importance. "I suppose I don't need it anymore." That thought would take some getting used to. She leaned against the arm of the couch, considering. "It represented...I don't know. Me taking my life back, maybe. Made me feel less vulnerable." Hadn't conquered her fears, hadn't come close, but it had given her a way to combat them.

"At least you took the time to learn to use it."

"Wouldn't have been much point, would there, to buy a gun and still not be able to defend myself?" Her throat clenched then. She'd never thought that she'd be using it to save someone, though. And the memory of Niko holding his weapon on Jack would take a long time to dissipate.

"I should probably tell you that some guys would get all macho at the thought of a girl saving their lives."

She watched him carefully. He was kidding. She was almost certain of it. "I'm sure you're more enlightened than that."

He gave a slow nod. "As it happens, I am. I can appreciate the instinct. Especially since I came damn close to throwing myself in front of you when it looked like he was going to squeeze a shot off."

Her knees went weak at the thought. "That would have been incredibly stupid."

"That's the thing about instinct." There was a heat in his eyes that was warming her from the inside out. "No thought involved."

Lindsay watched, mesmerized, as he sauntered toward her.

"Like the instinct I had the first time I met you." He stopped in front of her.

"To try every conceivable way to get me into bed?"

He smiled easily, reached for her hand. "There was that. But I'm talking about my highly developed cop instinct. Honed by years on these dangerous streets." She smiled a little at his droll tone. "Those instincts told me there's more to this lady than meets the eye." His thumb skated across her knuckles caressingly. "I thought, *I wonder what she's trying to hide behind those prim clothes.*"

It was difficult to concentrate when nerve endings were bursting to life beneath his touch. "Ah…so that's what you were looking for when you got me naked."

He chuckled. "I've got an inquiring mind. And a noble streak, too." He gave a tug and she was on her feet, in his arms with dizzying speed. "See, I feel an obligation to keep you off the streets. A woman like you…packing a concealed weapon. You're a threat to society."

"Very sacrificing of you."

His arms tightened around her and he bent his head to nip at her neck. "You oughta know from our first meeting that's the kind of guy I am. Nothing but give, give, give."

He laved the slight sting on her neck with his tongue. His closeness seemed to wipe her mind clean, and she was finding it difficult to think. And needed to, quite desperately.

"We've… Five days…" The rest of her statement was lost for the moment when his lips moved to her jaw and made a whisper-soft string of kisses to her ear.

"That we've known each other, I mean." She shuddered, when he took her earlobe between his teeth, worried it gently. "We've only known each other five days."

"Time's an interesting concept. A few instants can seem like a lifetime. Like when I went upstairs and saw Rassi with a gun to your head." A note of hardness entered his voice. "A lot can become clear in a moment like that."

It could, she knew. She tipped her head back, considered him. Because some things had crystallized for her when she'd fumbled to load that gun. Praying she had the guts to use it. Afraid that she wouldn't.

"I figure a woman on the run for three years isn't one to waste any more time than she has to. That's why I'm telling you now that I love you."

Her heart gave one dizzying spin in her chest. His expression had gone sober. His gaze searching. "I think you love me, too, but if you're the type to want a man to grovel a bit, I suppose I can wait to hear you say it."

"I do love you." She stopped, tried to find the words to explain her hesitation.

"But…" he prompted.

"I spent the last three years trying to play it safe. To curb that wild streak that has caused me nothing but trouble." She shook her head in bemusement as she studied him. "There is nothing remotely tame about you."

"We'll tame each other," he vowed. He lowered his mouth to hers, hovered a fraction of an inch above it. "And from now on, when we take a walk on the wild side, it'll be together."

* * * * *

There's more thrilling romance coming your way from
Kylie Brant and Alpha Squad!
Don't miss book 3, TERMS OF ATTRACTION,
in July 2009.
Only from Silhouette Romantic Suspense.

*Celebrate 60 years of pure reading pleasure with
Harlequin® Books!*

*Harlequin Romance® is celebrating by showering you
with DIAMOND BRIDES in February 2009.
Six stories that promise to bring a touch of sparkle to
your life, with diamond proposals and dazzling
weddings, sparkling brides and gorgeous grooms!*

*Enjoy a sneak peek at Caroline Anderson's
TWO LITTLE MIRACLES,
available February 2009 from Harlequin Romance®.*

'I'VE FOUND HER.'

Max froze.

It was what he'd been waiting for since June, but now—now he was almost afraid to voice the question. His heart stalling, he leaned slowly back in his chair and scoured the investigator's face for clues. 'Where?' he asked, and his voice sounded rough and unused, like a rusty hinge.

'In Suffolk. She's living in a cottage.'

Living. His heart crashed back to life, and he sucked in a long, slow breath. All these months he'd feared—

'Is she well?'

'Yes, she's well.'

He had to force himself to ask the next question. 'Alone?'

The man paused. 'No. The cottage belongs to a man called John Blake. He's working away at the moment, but he comes and goes.'

God. He felt sick. So sick he hardly registered the next few words, but then gradually they sank in. 'She's got *what?*'

'Babies. Twin girls. They're eight months old.'

'Eight—?' he echoed under his breath. 'They must be his.'

He was thinking out loud, but the P.I. heard and corrected him.

'Apparently not. I gather they're hers. She's been there since mid-January last year, and they were born during the summer—June, the woman in the post office thought. She was more than helpful. I think there's been a certain amount of speculation about their relationship.'

He'd just bet there had. God, he was going to kill her. Or Blake. Maybe both of them.

'Of course, looking at the dates, she was presumably pregnant when she left you, so they could be yours, or she could have been having an affair with this Blake character before...'

He glared at the unfortunate P.I. 'Just stick to your job. I can do the math,' he snapped, swallowing the unpalatable possibility that she'd been unfaithful to him before she'd left. 'Where is she? I want the address.'

'It's all in here,' the man said, sliding a large envelope across the desk to him. 'With my invoice.'

'I'll get it seen to. Thank you.'

'If there's anything else you need, Mr Gallagher, any further information—'

'I'll be in touch.'

'The woman in the post office told me Blake was away at the moment, if that helps,' he added quietly, and opened the door.

Max stared down at the envelope, hardly daring to open it, but when the door clicked softly shut behind the P.I., he eased up the flap, tipped it and felt his breath jam in his throat as the photos spilled out over the desk.

Oh, lord, she looked gorgeous. Different, though. It took him a moment to recognise her, because she'd grown her hair, and it was tied back in a ponytail, making her look younger and somehow freer. The blond highlights were gone, and it was back to its natural soft golden-brown, with a little curl in the end of the ponytail that he wanted to thread his finger through and tug, just gently, to draw her back to him.

Crazy. She'd put on a little weight, but it suited her. She looked well and happy and beautiful, but oddly, considering how desperate he'd been for news of her for the past year—one year, three weeks and two days, to be exact—it wasn't only Julia who held his attention after the initial shock. It was the babies sitting side by side in a supermarket trolley. Two identical and absolutely beautiful little girls.

* * * * *

When Max Gallagher hires a P.I. to find his estranged wife, Julia, he discovers she's not alone— she has twin baby girls, and they might be his. Now workaholic Max has just two weeks to prove that he can be a wonderful husband and father to the family he wants to treasure.

Look for TWO LITTLE MIRACLES
by Caroline Anderson,
available February 2009
from Harlequin Romance®.

CELEBRATE
60 YEARS
OF PURE READING PLEASURE
WITH HARLEQUIN®!

We'll be spotlighting a different series
every month throughout 2009
to celebrate our 60th anniversary.

Look for Harlequin® Romance in February!

Harlequin® Romance is celebrating by showering
you with Diamond Brides in February 2009.

Six stories that promise to bring a touch of sparkle to
your life, with diamond proposals and dazzling weddings,
sparkling brides and gorgeous grooms!

Collect all six books in February 2009,
featuring *Two Little Miracles* by Caroline Anderson.

*Look for the Diamond Brides miniseries
in February 2009!*

HARLEQUIN® *Romance*®

This February the Harlequin® Romance series
will feature six Diamond Brides stories featuring
diamond proposals and gorgeous grooms.

Share your dream wedding proposal and you could WIN!

The most romantic entry will win a diamond
necklace and will inspire a proposal in one of
our upcoming Diamond Grooms books in 2010.

In 100 words or less, tell us the most romantic
way that you dream of being proposed to.

For more information, and to enter
the Diamond Brides Proposal contest, please visit
www.DiamondBridesProposal.com

Or mail your entry to us at:
IN THE U.S.: 3010 Walden Ave., P.O. Box 9069, Buffalo, NY 14269-9069
IN CANADA: 225 Duncan Mill Road, Don Mills, ON M3B 3K9

REQUEST YOUR FREE BOOKS!

2 FREE NOVELS PLUS 2 FREE GIFTS!

Silhouette® Romantic

SUSPENSE

Sparked by Danger, Fueled by Passion!

YES! Please send me 2 FREE Silhouette® Romantic Suspense novels and my 2 FREE gifts (gifts are worth about $10). After receiving them, if I don't wish to receive any more books, I can return the shipping statement marked "cancel." If I don't cancel, I will receive 4 brand-new novels every month and be billed just $4.24 per book in the U.S. or $4.99 per book in Canada, plus 25¢ shipping and handling per book plus applicable taxes, if any*. That's a savings of at least 15% off the cover price! I understand that accepting the 2 free books and gifts places me under no obligation to buy anything. I can always return a shipment and cancel at any time. Even if I never buy another book from Silhouette, the two free books and gifts are mine to keep forever.

240 SDN EEX6   340 SDN EEYJ

Name	(PLEASE PRINT)

Address	Apt. #

City	State/Prov.	Zip/Postal Code

Signature (if under 18, a parent or guardian must sign)

Mail to the Silhouette Reader Service:

IN U.S.A.: P.O. Box 1867, Buffalo, NY 14240-1867
IN CANADA: P.O. Box 609, Fort Erie, Ontario L2A 5X3

Not valid to current subscribers of Silhouette Romantic Suspense books.

**Want to try two free books from another line?
Call 1-800-873-8635 or visit www.morefreebooks.com.**

* Terms and prices subject to change without notice. N.Y. residents add applicable sales tax. Canadian residents will be charged applicable provincial taxes and GST. Offer not valid in Quebec. This offer is limited to one order per household. All orders subject to approval. Credit or debit balances in a customer's account(s) may be offset by any other outstanding balance owed by or to the customer. Please allow 4 to 6 weeks for delivery. Offer available while quantities last.

Your Privacy: Silhouette is committed to protecting your privacy. Our Privacy Policy is available online at www.eHarlequin.com or upon request from the Reader Service. From time to time we make our lists of customers available to reputable third parties who may have a product or service of interest to you. If you would prefer we not share your name and address, please check here. ☐

SRS08R

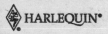

Romantic
SUSPENSE

COMING NEXT MONTH

#1547 SCANDAL IN COPPER LAKE—Marilyn Pappano
When Anamaria Duquesne returns to Copper Lake to discover the truth about her mother's death and her still-missing baby sister, she doesn't count on running into Robbie Calloway. Suspecting her of being a con artist, Robbie agrees to keep an eye on Anamaria, but he can't help entertaining feelings for her. And a relationship with Anamaria would be anything but easy....

#1548 A HERO OF HER OWN—Carla Cassidy
The Coltons: Family First
From the moment she arrives in town, Jewel Mayfair catches the attention of veterinarian Quinn Logan. They're both overcoming tragic pasts, but as Jewel lets down her guard to give in to passion with Quinn, mysterious events make her question her choices. Should she take a second chance on love, or is Quinn the last man she should trust?

#1549 THE REDEMPTION OF RAFE DIAZ—Maggie Price
Dates with Destiny
Businesswoman Allie Fielding never thought she'd see Rafe Diaz again—at least not on the outside of a prison cell! But when Allie stumbles over the body of a murdered customer, the now-exonerated P.I. she helped put behind bars shows up to question her. His investigation stirs up a past Rafe thought was behind him—and unlocks a passion that could put them both at risk.

#1550 HEART AT RISK—Ana Leigh
Bishop's Heroes
A family was the furthest thing from Kurt Bolen's mind, yet when he discovers he has a son, he'll do whatever it takes to make the boy and his mother his own. But someone is after Kurt, and in the midst of rekindling their romance, he and Maddie must band together to protect their son and fight for their future.

SRSCNMBPA0109